An Idea  Brain...An Idea She Tried To Squash.

Really, she did. Because the idea was unthinkable. Reprehensible. Immoral. What she had in mind was no way to repay all the kindness and patience Cooper had shown to her and her son. He might very well have saved both their lives last night.

She looked again at the line where the birth certificate application asked for the name of Andrew's father.

As if they had a mind of their own, Katie's fingers gripped more tightly the pen in her hand, and she watched with an almost detached fascination as they wrote out, in big, block letters...
C-O-O-P-E-R D-U-G-A-N.

Dear Reader,

Welcome to Silhouette Desire, where you can discover the answers to *all* your romantic questions. Such as…

Q. *What would you think if you discovered the man you love has a secret identity—as a movie star?*

A. That's what happens to the heroine of August's MAN OF THE MONTH, *Don't Fence Me In* by award-winning writer Kathleen Korbel.

Q. *What would you do if you were pregnant, in labor and snowbound with a sexy—but panicked—stranger?*

A. Discover the answer in *Father on the Brink*, the conclusion to Elizabeth Bevarly's FROM HERE TO PATERNITY series.

Q. *Suppose you had to have a marriage of convenience?*

A. Maybe you'd behave like the heroine in Barbara McMahon's *Bride of a Thousand Days*.

Q. *How could you talk a man into fathering your child…no strings attached?*

A. Learn how in Susan Crosby's *Baby Fever!*

Q. *Would you ever marry a stranger?*

A. You might, if he was the hero of Sara Orwig's *The Bride's Choice*.

Q. *What does it take to lasso a sexy cowboy?*

A. Find out in Shawna Delacorte's *Cowboy Dreaming*.

Silhouette Desire…where all your questions are answered and your romantic dreams can come true.

Until next month, happy reading!

Lucia Macro

Senior Editor

Please address questions and book requests to:
Silhouette Reader Service
U.S.: 3010 Walden Ave., P.O. Box 1325, Buffalo, NY 14269
Canadian: P.O. Box 609, Fort Erie, Ont. L2A 5X3

ELIZABETH
BEVARLY
FATHER ON THE BRINK

SILHOUETTE *Desire*®
Published by Silhouette Books
America's Publisher of Contemporary Romance

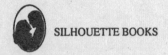

SILHOUETTE BOOKS

ISBN 0-373-76016-7

FATHER ON THE BRINK

This edition published by arrangement with Harlequin Books S.A.

® and TM are trademarks of Harlequin Books S.A., used under license.
Trademarks indicated with ® are registered in the United States Patent
and Trademark Office, the Canadian Trade Marks Office and in other
countries.

Printed in U.S.A.

ELIZABETH BEVARLY

is an honors graduate of the University of Louisville and achieved her dream of writing full-time before she even turned thirty! At heart she is also an avid voyager who once helped navigate a friend's thirty-five-foot sailboat across the Bermuda Triangle. "I really love to travel," says this self-avowed beach bum. "To me, it's the best education a person can give to herself." Her dream is to one day have her own sailboat, a beautifully renovated older model forty-two footer, and to enjoy the freedom and tranquillity sea-faring can bring. Elizabeth likes to think she has a lot in common with the characters she creates, people who know love and life go hand in hand. And she's getting some firsthand experience with maternity, as well—she and her husband recently welcomed their firstborn baby, a son.

For Teresa Hill/Sally Tyler Hayes
and
Barbara Samuel/Ruth Wind

Thanks for being there when I needed you.

And with thanks to my
New Jersey and Pennsylvania connections:

Gin, April and Hannah
and
Judy and Sharyn.

Much obliged, you guys.

One

It was a blizzard of unprecedented proportions, even by northeastern standards. Cooper Dugan tried his damnedest to squint through the splashes of white that pelted his windshield, pressed his foot against the clutch and downshifted into first. The cold March wind whipped easily through the plastic doors and windows of the four-wheel drive Jeep, chilling even more thoroughly his already frozen nose, seeping through his leather gloves to numb his fingers to the bone.

He fumbled for the thermos of coffee he'd been clutching between his knees for most of the ride and unscrewed the lid, then sipped carefully from the lip without bothering with the plastic cup. The liquid was hotter than he'd expected it to be, and he burned his tongue, dribbling a good portion of the dark brown brew down his chin and throat, under his wool muffler and into the neck of the sweatshirt he wore beneath his leather college baseball jacket. Uttering a vicious and colorful oath, he scrubbed a hand over the bottom half of his face and growled low.

"Hell of a way to spend a Saturday night," he muttered to no one in particular.

He was supposed to have been off this weekend, he reminded himself mercilessly. He was supposed to have been out on a date, at this very minute, with that new nurse in cardiology—the big brunette with the heart-shaped fanny, and breasts that just begged a man to cushion his head upon them and rest for a while. He was supposed to be enjoying himself a little bit after having worked eighteen days straight without a break. Instead, he was playing Good Samaritan to the City of Brotherly Love, responding to a cry for help from the mayor, who wasn't even paying Cooper for his time.

Hey, it wasn't *his* fault the weather guys had overlooked and underestimated what had become the biggest and most crippling snowfall in Pennsylvania's history, was it? It wasn't *his* fault they'd all said, "No, don't worry, it's going to go way north of us." It wasn't *his* fault the snowplows hadn't even had a chance to make it out of the city garage. And it wasn't *his* fault—or his problem, for that matter—that a bunch of local citizens were having trouble getting the medical attention they required on a day-to-day basis.

Hey, he didn't even *live* in Philadelphia. He was a Jersey boy, born and bred, the Pennsauken apartment he lived in now virtually a stone's throw away from the house where he'd spent his childhood.

So what the hell was he doing out here freezing his butt off, battling a temperamental Jeep to keep it on the road, eating stale Twinkies, and spilling coffee down his shirt?

"No rest for the wicked, I guess," he complained to himself. "Or for paramedics, either."

He jotted down a mental note to himself: *Hey, Coop, next time something like this happens, and the city across the Delaware River gets buried under snow, and some public official makes a public appeal to any citizen possessing a four-wheel drive vehicle and even the most rudimentary first-aid skills . . . the next time something like this happens, be in Barbados, okay?*

"Cooper, honey, you still out there?"

The crackly voice buzzed over the radio he'd tossed onto the passenger seat earlier that evening, and, reluctant to take his eyes off of the road—what little he could see of it— Cooper groped around for a minute before finally finding it.

"Yeah, Patsy, I'm still with you," he replied after squeezing the Talk button.

"Where you at?"

Cooper chuckled and tried to see some kind of vague landmark through the snow. Finally, he lifted the radio to his mouth again and said, "I have no idea."

"Well, give me a rough estimate."

Cooper sighed, slowed the Jeep to a crawl and noted a row of orangey-looking town houses edging the tree-lined street. "I think I'm in Chestnut Hill," he told Patsy. "Looks like Chestnut Hill anyway, and that's the way I was headed. Sorta. There are trees. Where else in downtown Philly am I going to see trees?"

He heard the dispatcher expel a sound of relief. "Sounds like Chestnut Hill to me. Okay, that's great, Cooper. I've got another run for you." A pause, then, "I can't read Don's handwriting very well, but it looks like you've got a kidney patient—a sixty-seven-year-old male—who couldn't make dialysis this afternoon. You better get over there right quick."

"Quick," he mumbled to himself. "Yeah, right."

He knew the dispatcher, like everyone else scrambling to work through this situation, had been pressed into duty when she had other things to do—like keeping herself and her family warm and safe. But Cooper's patience was shrinking as his tension and need for sleep increased.

Already today, he'd ferried a four-year-old with a broken ankle to the hospital, cringing at the little guy's pain-filled howling all the way. He'd resuscitated a major coronary after the eighty-year-old woman had tried to keep ahead of the snow in shoveling her driveway. He'd run a batch of prescriptions from a local pharmacy to four very needy people in utterly opposite corners of town. He'd even rushed a golden retriever to a veterinarian.

Organization at the dispatch source, it seemed, was the biggest casualty of the blizzard so far.

He pressed the Talk button again. "Patsy," he began as patiently as he could. " 'Right quick' isn't an option at the moment. At this point, with the snow coming down like it is, I'll be lucky if I can get to the old guy by daybreak tomorrow."

"Just get there," she snapped back, obviously stretched as thin as Cooper was. She rattled off an address that he hoped like hell he would remember, because there was no way he was taking his hand off the steering wheel long enough to write anything down.

It took him nearly half an hour to reach the street that wound up being only a block from what had been his location when Patsy had assigned him the duty. After his sixth pass up the block in question, Cooper finally found the town house he was looking for. At least, he thought it was the one he was looking for. He parked in the middle of the street, unconcerned that anyone was going to hit or strip the vehicle. After all, only idiots like him were out on a night like this, right?

Automatically, he reached behind the passenger seat for the well-stocked first-aid kit he always carried with him. Then he pushed the Jeep door open, pulled the hood of his sweatshirt up over his head, tucked his body in as well as he could against the wind and snow, and jogged toward the house.

* * *

Katherine Winslow had been packing for a very long trip to Anywhere-But-Here when her water had broken. She'd gasped when she'd felt the warm rush of fluid slide down her legs and soak the pants of her maternity overalls, then had stared down at the clear liquid pooling around her feet with much dismay. It had been a troubling development, to say the least, coming as it did three weeks before her due date, in the middle of the worst blizzard in Pennsylvania history, and right on the heels of her discovery that her husband wasn't who he claimed to be—including her husband.

There was nothing like having a man's wife show up at your front door to tell you that you weren't. The man's wife, that is.

Now as Katherine lay curled up in a ball in the middle of the king-size bed she'd been sharing with a stranger for months, clutching her abdomen as spasms of pain rocked her, she had no idea what to do.

William would know, she thought. If he'd been home, instead of traveling on business—or, at least, on what he had *told* her was business—William would know exactly what to do. He'd be taking good care of her. Just as he'd been taking good care of her since the day she'd met him. Just like a husband was supposed to do for his wife.

Except that William wasn't her husband, Katherine reminded herself, squeezing her eyes shut as another cramp rippled over her belly. He'd somehow neglected to mention that he was already married when he'd walked her down the aisle at Reverend Ryan's Chapel O'Love in Las Vegas nearly a year ago.

One thing he *was,* though, was the father of her baby. A baby who, if Katherine had her way, would never, ever, meet up with the man who'd sired him. Unfortunately, it looked like William had other ideas.

But right now, that was the least of her problems. She'd been in labor for hours and was completely unprepared for whatever lay ahead. William had discouraged her from taking prenatal classes, telling her she'd have the best doctors and nurses attending her when her time came, and they'd be the ones who needed to know what to do, not her. And although she had done some reading, right now she could remember nothing of what the books had instructed her to do.

She should probably call someone, she thought, glancing toward the telephone that sat on the nightstand near her head. But what few friends she had in Philadelphia had been William's before they'd been hers. So word of his son's imminent birth would get back to him, wherever he was, and then the man who wasn't her husband would come rushing to be by her side. Which was the last place she wanted to find him. Another pain sliced through her midsection, and she cried out, wondering what could possibly make this situation worse than it already was.

As if playing a very bad joke, the lights flickered above her, then went out completely.

Katherine rolled to her other side and wished she would wake up from what was becoming a truly terrible nightmare. Even in darkness, the beauty that surrounded her seemed to scoff at her. William had furnished their Chestnut Hill town house with the finest antiques and Oriental carpets money could buy. She had always been so grateful that her child would be born into wealth, that the tiny baby growing inside her would never have to know the hardship and poverty she had known growing up.

But there were many kinds of poverty, she now understood. And William suffered from the basest kind. Emotional poverty. Moral poverty. Poverty of the soul.

He wasn't her husband, she reminded herself again. Which was good, now that she thought about it. Because that would give her a little more leverage when he came to take her son away from her.

She cried out as a new kind of pain shook her, and for the first time, she became afraid—really afraid. Afraid that something was going to go wrong with the baby, afraid of being alone for the rest of her life, afraid that no matter how hard she tried, she'd already ruined things irreparably.

She splayed her hands open over her belly, the closest thing she could manage to an embrace of her unborn son. "I'm sorry," she whispered as tears stung her eyes. "Oh, sweetie, I'm so, so sorry."

Cooper pounded the door with his closed fist for the third time, cursing Patsy with every other breath for giving him the wrong address. He punched the doorbell over and over and over, listening in helpless frustration. He was lifting his hand for one final knock when the radio in his pocket buzzed and crackled, and Patsy's voice came over the line.

"Cooper?"

He withdrew the two-way with a snarl and lifted it to his lips. "Yeah?"

"Um, sorry, hon, but I think I sent you on a wild goose chase."

He let every four-letter word he knew—and some more that he made up on the spot—parade across the front of his brain before he responded quietly, "What?"

"Uh, yeah. That dialysis note was from this afternoon. The guy's been in and is safely back home now. I'm sorry. You don't need to be where you are."

Cooper was about to agree with her, was about to tell Patsy that where he actually *needed* to be was lying in the arms of a willing woman who cradled a big snifter of very expensive, very *warm,* brandy beneath his lips, when he heard an almost unearthly feminine scream erupt on the other side of the door he'd been about to pound off its hinges.

Immediately, he dropped his hand to the knob and twisted hard. But it wouldn't budge. Another scream raged at him from inside, and without thinking, Cooper lifted his metal first-aid kit and brought it crashing down on the knob. Over and over again, he repeated the action, until he'd bashed what had been an elegant collection of brass curlicues and engravings into a twisted metal mess. Finally, the entire fixture failed, and he shoved his shoulder against the door, hard.

Inside, the house was dark. Only the reflection of a street lamp on the other side of the street colliding with the quickly falling snow prevented the foyer from being completely black. He heard someone gasping for breath somewhere beyond his vision, and assumed it to be the woman who had screamed. Cautiously, he took a few steps forward.

"Hello?" he called out. "Who's there? Are you all right?"

His only reply was a stifled, disembodied groan.

"Hel-looo?" he tried again. "It's okay. Don't be scared. I'm a paramedic. I can help you."

At first, he thought the woman had stopped breathing, so silent did the room become. His heartbeat quickened, rushing blood to warm the parts of his body he'd begun to fear had frozen. He pushed the hood of his sweatshirt back off his head, then raked his fingers through his snow-dampened, overly long, pale blond hair. He held his own breath, waiting for something, some indication that he wasn't too late to remedy whatever had gone wrong in this house.

Finally, a tiny, feminine voice called from the other side of the room, "H-h-help me?"

Cooper took a few more strides in the direction from which the question had come. "Yeah, I can help you. Just tell me where you are."

"H-help. Please."

He opened his first-aid kit and pulled out a flashlight, switching it on to throw a wide ray of white light all around the room. The hazy halo finally settled on a woman in the corner. A woman whose dark hair was soaking wet with perspiration in spite of the chill in the house, and whose huge, gray eyes were terrified. A woman who was clutching a belly distended in the very late stages of pregnancy.

"Oh, no," Cooper muttered. "No, no, no. Not this. Anything but this."

The woman lifted her hand to him. "Help," she whispered, her voice sounding thin and weak and exhausted. "Please . . . my baby. Help my baby."

He threw his head back to stare into the darkness above him. Great. This was just great. Of all the damned, stupid, crazy luck, he had to wind up with a home birth. Because there was no way he was going to try to get this lady to the hospital. The only thing worse than a home delivery was a back seat of a Jeep in a blizzard delivery.

He sighed his resignation to the situation, set his flashlight and first-aid kit on a nearby coffee table and looked at the woman in the corner again.

"Are you here all alone?" he asked her.

She nodded. "Husband's . . . out of town."

He scrubbed a hand over his face, a singularly troubled gesture. "I don't think I'm going to be able to get you to the hospital in time. Looks like we're going to have to deliver that baby right here. Is that okay with you?"

She nodded weakly, but said nothing.

Cooper felt the chill winter wind sweep past him from behind and went back to close the front door. He spied a fireplace upon his return, noting gratefully that it was already laid for a fire and needed only the flick of a match to provide some much needed warmth. There was a box of matches on the mantel, settled amid a half dozen framed photographs of the woman who was crumpled into a ball in the corner of the room. He ignored the pictures, scratched a couple of matches on the side of the box and tossed them into the kindling. Within moments, the flames began to flicker upward into the wood, bathing the room in a faint yellow glow, warming his face and hands.

He turned back to the woman. "Okay. That'll get us started. We'll have to deliver the baby down here, since I assume there's no heat anywhere else in the house. We're going to need some clean sheets, some water.... I think I have everything else we'll need in my kit. So, where do you keep all that stuff, and where can I wash up?"

Katherine stared back at the huge apparition that had come out of nowhere, feeling anything but relieved. In the weak ray of the flashlight, with the scant flicker of flames in the fireplace illuminating him with an odd play of light and shadow, the only impression she had of him was that he was big, broad and blond. His voice, rich and masculine and anything but comforting, told her he was none too thrilled to be acting as midwife. But he'd said he was a paramedic. That meant he had to know something about childbirth, right? Certainly more than she knew herself.

The pain in her midsection seemed to have abated some after pelting her repeatedly with one severe spasm after another, and she took advantage of the opportunity to inhale a few deep, calming breaths. When she trusted her voice to remain steady, she gave the man the information he'd requested, then pointed toward the kitchen and told him he could wash up in there. Immediately, he disappeared into the direction she'd indicated, and Katherine slumped back against the wall. She had changed into a nightgown after her water had broken, but the fluid continued to leak from her in a steady flow. Now the white cotton fabric was cold and damp. She wanted to be near the fire.

She was struggling to stand when the man returned and saw her intentions, so he helped her to her feet and led her to the sofa. Again she was struck by his size and solidity. She told herself if she were smart, she'd be afraid of him. But Katherine had never been any too intelligent where men were concerned, as evidenced by her current predicament. And for some reason, in spite of his size and demeanor and the fact that he was a complete stranger, this man didn't frighten her at all.

"Where did you come from?" she managed to ask him as he settled her on the sofa. "How did you know I was here?" She couldn't quite stop herself from asking further, "Did...did William send you?"

The man had turned his back to her and was busying himself with what looked like a very substantial first-aid kit. "Who's William?" he asked, though his mind didn't seem to be on the question.

"My...my husband. Did he...are you here because of him?"

The man shook his head, but still seemed to be preoccupied with making the proper preparations for bringing her son into the world. "Nope," he said. "It's just sheer, dumb luck that linked us up, lady. Sheer, dumb luck."

She was about to ask him to elaborate on that, but a faint pain rippled up inside her again, and she squeezed her eyes shut, clenching her teeth together in an effort to ease the ache a bit.

"How long has the power been out?" the man asked her when he spun back around to look at her.

She dropped her hand to her belly, rubbing at another, less intense, contraction. "I don't know. It was still daylight when my water broke—about four, four-thirty maybe. What time is it now?"

The man turned his wristwatch toward the dim glow of the flashlight. "Just past nine. You've been in labor for five hours?"

Katherine thought for a moment. The pains hadn't really started until some time after her water broke, but for the life of her, she couldn't quite remember now how long. "I don't know," she said again.

The man dropped to his haunches before her, bringing his face level with hers. She was able to tell a little bit more about him when he was up close this way, the growing light from the fire illuminating one side of his face, but not much more. At least one good cheekbone, she noted. And at least one vivid green eye. And a pair of lips, one half of which anyway, that were full and beautiful and still managed to be very, very masculine.

He started to extend his hand toward hers, then seemed to think better of it, and wove his fingers together on one knee. "What's your name?" he asked her.

She opened her mouth to tell him the truth, then realized the truth was in fact a lie. She wasn't Katherine Winslow. There was no Katherine Winslow. William had made her that with his farce of a wedding. Without him, she had no idea who she would be now. So she told the man, "I'm Katie Brennan." It was what she had been called in her other life, a million years ago. And it seemed to suit her now.

"Katie Brennan," the man repeated.

He smiled, and for the first time in what seemed a very long time, Katie felt a warming sense of relief seep into her. This time when he reached out for her, he carried through, taking her hand in his.

"Nice to meet you, Katie," he said. "I'm Cooper. Cooper Dugan. And, like I said, I'm a paramedic. But I'll be honest with you. I've never delivered a baby before. I mean, I know what to do—pretty much—but I've never actually..." His voice trailed off when he seemed to detect her growing sense of misgiving. "Is this your first?" he asked quietly.

She nodded, her sudden conviction about feeling safe faltering a little with his announcement.

He nodded back. "Then I guess we have something in common."

She was about to say something else when the pains flared up again, bursting out of nowhere with even more intensity than before. Katie cried out, crushing with what she was sure was bruising strength the hand that Cooper Dugan had offered her in comfort.

It was going to be a long night.

She didn't realize she had spoken her thought aloud until Cooper nodded in agreement and said, "Yeah, it sure is."

She watched as he reached behind himself for his jacket, plucked a two-way radio from one pocket, and spoke into it. "Patsy," he said with a sigh, "this is Coop. Better take me off the dispatch list. I'm going to be, um, indisposed for a little while."

Two

Eventually, night became morning. And by the time it did, the blizzard had tapered off into an almost magical-looking snowfall, the power in Katie's house had come back on, and Cooper had helped to deliver a bouncing baby boy.

The knowledge of that startled him still.

In spite of the restoration of electricity, a fire continued to crackle happily in the fireplace, and the lights were dimmed low. He sat in his ancient blue jeans and Kmart special T-shirt on the floor of Katie's big, expensive town house, amid more opulence and luxury than he'd imagined was possible. And he ignored it all to stare instead at a sleeping mother and child for whom he felt, at least partially, responsible.

He thought about the tradition that other cultures embraced, about how when a person saved another person's life, he became responsible for whomever he'd rescued. He supposed the same must hold true when a person brought another person into the world to begin with. That was the only reason Cooper could conceive why he felt such a strong tie to the little guy tucked safely and snugly in his mother's arms.

He studied the baby's mother, too. For some reason, Cooper also felt responsible for Katie Brennan now. She lay on the floor with her upper back and head supported by a pile of pillows, naked amid a tangle of sheets. Purple crescents smudged her eyes, and her dark hair was shoved back from her forehead in a heap of wet snarls. He knew nothing about her other than her name and address. Yet he couldn't quite chase away the sensation that he was bound to her irrevocably.

His gaze dropped to the ring encircling the fourth finger of her left hand. Studded with diamonds, it was the kind of wedding band a man gave to a woman he intended to keep forever. Certainly, it was a far cry from anything Cooper could ever hope to afford for a woman himself, regardless of how much he might love her. Katie Brennan was obviously a woman accustomed to a way of life vastly different from his own.

Not that it mattered, he told himself. The woman was married, after all, and tied to her husband with a bond far more significant and lasting than the one represented by the ring on her finger. She had a child. Her husband's child. And nothing on earth could shatter a bond like that.

Cooper cupped a hand to the back of his neck and rubbed hard. *Long night* hadn't begun to describe what he and Katie had just been through. And if he was this tired, he could only imagine how she must feel after a grueling session like that. She'd screamed, and he'd hollered, and they'd both sworn like drunken sailors. She'd pushed and shoved and heaved and cried. He'd cajoled and threatened and bribed and heartened. And sometime just before the sun began to stain the sky with pink and yellow, Andrew Cooper Brennan had been born.

It had been Katie's idea—no, her demand—that her son carry Cooper's first name for his middle one. Andrew, she said, had been her father's name. And when Cooper had asked how her husband was going to feel about his son carrying a stranger's name, Katie had smiled sadly through her exhaustion and told Cooper he was less of a stranger to her than her husband was. Before he'd had a chance to get her to clarify that, she'd drifted into a sound slumber, and he'd decided she must have been touched with a bit of postpartum delirium and hadn't known what she was talking about.

Not for the first time since she'd fallen asleep, his gaze wandered up to the mantel, to the scattered collection of photographs. Katie with her arms circling a collie's neck, both of them grinning from ear to ear. Katie smiling shyly from beneath the broad brim of a straw hat, a tranquil, turquoise sea behind her. Katie with her head bent to and partially obscured by a bouquet of yellow roses. Katie with a good-looking man Cooper assumed was her husband, the two of them standing beside a sleek black Jaguar, laughing as if they'd just played the biggest joke in the world on someone.

And another photograph that seemed oddly out of place, yet more suited to Katie than any of the others. It was a picture of her as a young teenager, standing on the steps of what looked like a sagging farmhouse, a man and woman situated like fence posts behind her, each one with a hand on her shoulder. The only one in the picture who was smiling was Katie. But even hers was a sad, almost wistful expression.

Cooper's gaze fell to her sleeping so near him, and again he couldn't quite shake the feeling that he was somehow responsible for her now. For her and her baby both. The realization was still flooding over him when Katie opened her eyes and smiled.

"Good morning," she said softly, obviously no better rested for her sleep than she had been when she'd closed her eyes two hours ago.

Cooper smiled back. His voice was scarcely a whisper as he replied, "Good morning to you, too."

She looked down at the baby in her arms, who awoke and whimpered a bit before snuggling into her breast. He rooted around, and Katie chuckled, trying to get him properly positioned. Only after a number of trials and errors did the baby finally affix himself onto her nipple and begin a greedy suckle.

"I'm going to have to find someone who knows more about this breastfeeding business than I do," she said when she met Cooper's gaze again. "I don't think either Andrew or I have a clue how to go about it."

For the first time, Cooper noted that her speech carried just the hint of a southern accent of some kind. Obviously, she wasn't from the tristate area originally.

He shrugged off her concern. "There will be someone at the hospital who can help you out. Or they can at least give you a referral."

Her smile faltered. "Hospital?"

He raised his arms over his head and arched his back into a stretch. "Sure," he said absently when he'd completed it. "Now that the snow's letting up, the plows ought to be able to get through. And seeing as how so many wealthy taxpayers live right here in Chestnut Hill, your neighborhood will probably be one of the first to get plowed." He hoped none of the edge he felt when he uttered the last of his comments found its way into his voice.

"But—" She hesitated, leaving her objection unuttered.

"But what?" he asked. "Aren't you anxious to get to the hospital to make sure everything's okay with you and the baby?"

She shook her head. "I know everything's okay."

"How do you know?"

"I just do."

Cooper nodded, but found it more than a little strange that she would be so reluctant to get to a medical facility. "Yeah, well, it might not be a bad idea to have the two of you checked out anyway. Just to be sure. I called the hospital a little while ago, and they're sending an ambulance ASAP. Of course, with all that snow out there, ASAP isn't going to be as fast as it usually would."

If possible, her face became even paler than it already was. "You did what?"

"I called the hospital. An ambulance should be here in a couple of hours to collect you and little Andrew. It's standard procedure. What's the problem?"

Katie shook her head and wondered what she was going to do now. The problem was that going to the hospital necessitated registering Andrew's birth and lots of questions about his father. She knew she was legally obligated to inform the state of a new arrival. Even if in doing so, she was providing an already well-armed monster with just the right weapon to take her baby away from her forever. Once William's name was on Andrew's birth certificate, his stable of overpaid, amoral attorneys would have everything they needed—in writing—to ensure that Katie never saw her son again.

"I can't go to the hospital," she said.

Cooper arched his brows in surprise. "Why not?"

"I just...I can't, Cooper. You have to call them back and tell them you made a mistake."

He gaped at her. "A mistake? Excuse me? What do you want me to do, call and say, 'Hi, this is Coop again. You know that baby I told you I delivered? Well, I was wrong. It was actually a pepperoni pizza that I delivered. Sorry about the mix-up.'"

She made a face at him. "No, of course not. But it's very important that Andrew and I not go to the hospital."

"Why?"

"We just can't," she snapped.

"Well, that's too bad," he snapped back. "Because you're both going to the hospital. And I intend to escort you every step of the way, just to make sure you don't get lost in the shuffle."

Katie opened her mouth to object again, then decided it would be fruitless to do so. She'd learned at some point during the night—when she kept insisting that she had changed her mind, and that she had decided she was *not* going to have this baby, no matter how much Cooper begged or threatened, and that was final—that the man simply wouldn't take no for an answer.

She glanced down at Andrew, who pulled hungrily at her breast. He was fat and pink and squirmy, and it hit Katie with the force of an aircraft carrier that she was entirely responsible for him. It was up to her to make sure no harm ever came to her son. It was up to her to be certain that he had the very best of everything she could offer him. It was up to her to see that he was safe and happy and free to live a good life. It was up to her to ensure that William Winslow never got his hands on his son.

Therefore, she had to be certain that she and Andrew were as physically fit as possible before they went into hiding.

Her gaze locked with Cooper's again. "All right. We'll go to the hospital."

He expelled a dubious sound of relief. "Well, thank you very much."

"You don't have to be sarcastic."

It occurred to Katie then that she was sitting in the middle of her living room completely naked with a man she scarcely knew. A man who had helped to bring her son into the world. A man who still carried smudges of her blood and her son's afterbirth on his T-shirt and jeans. The full realization and understanding of the intimacy she had shared with this stranger struck her, and she tugged the bed sheet up around her shoulders a little more.

Cooper's gaze flickered away from hers when she completed the action, and she thought she saw him blush. She smiled. It comforted her that, in spite of what they had gone through together, he could still respect her modesty.

"So..." he began, his voice quiet and a little bemused, "where's the dog?"

She frowned. "What dog?"

He gestured toward the photographs on the mantel. "The collie. Where is he?"

"She," Katie corrected him. "She belongs to an old friend of mine back in Las Vegas. I haven't seen either of them for nearly a year."

"You're from Las Vegas?" he asked, turning to look at her again. "That's funny. I could swear you have more of a southern accent."

She chuckled, then fumbled for a moment as she switched Andrew from her left breast to her right. When the baby was once more suckling happily, she looked up to find that Cooper had again looked away. Her smile grew broader.

"Still?" she asked. "I was hoping I'd managed to wipe it out completely."

"So you are from the south?"

She nodded. "Originally. Western Kentucky. I have a cousin who used to live in Vegas, though, so I went out there after I graduated from high school—that would have been about eight years ago—to make my fortune as a singer. Instead, I wound up working as a waitress. Until I met my... until I met William."

Cooper nodded but said nothing more.

"How about you?" she asked him.

"What about me?"

"Are you married? Got any kids?"

He laughed anxiously. "No way."

"Not the marrying kind, huh?"

"No."

The one-word answer, offered so quickly and certainly, told Katie just about everything she needed to know.

"Not the fathering kind, either," he added hastily, as if it were very important that he clarify his position on that, as well.

She nodded her understanding and told him, "Well, if you find yourself on your deathbed regretting that decision, you can rest easy knowing you're responsible for at least one child in the world. I really don't know what Andrew and I would have done if you hadn't shown up last night. I'll have to send a thank-you note to whoever got their wires crossed and sent you here by mistake."

He rubbed his eyes wearily as he told her, "No thanks necessary. I'm sure it was destiny."

Katie watched him covertly as he stretched again. If he was single, she thought, it certainly wasn't because no woman found any potential in him. During the night, she'd had neither the time, nor the inclination, to give much thought to her companion. But now, in the quiet light of the dawn, as her son—her *son!*—drifted off to sleep again in her arms, she took a moment to consider the man who had come to her out of the darkness and snow the night before.

He was, quite simply, beautiful. Beautifully formed, beautifully arranged, beautifully packaged. She wasn't sure she'd ever seen a man more attractive than Cooper Dugan. Nor had she ever met one so self-possessed. She had, understandably, been a bit anxious and panicky during the night. But Cooper had always managed to somehow keep her steady. She would never forget the sturdy, easy timbre of his voice as he'd coached her through Andrew's birth. Nor would she forget the strong hands that had so gently settled her baby on her belly the moment he'd emerged from inside her.

She shifted a little, wincing at the pain that shot through her with the motion. Not for the first time, Katie found herself wishing Cooper Dugan was the man who had fathered her son. Or, at least, a man like him. What could she possibly have been thinking to fall under William's spell? she wondered now. How could she have been so stupid?

She opened her mouth to say something to Cooper—though what she had meant for that something to be, she couldn't remember—when an almost debilitating fatigue overcame her. One minute, she was tired and weak, the next, she couldn't lift her hand to push her hair off of her forehead. "I need to sleep now," she managed to say before her eyelids fluttered down.

Though she wasn't absolutely certain, just before unconsciousness claimed her, she thought she heard him reply, "I understand."

And she found herself thinking, *Oh, Cooper, if only you could...*

Cooper watched Katie sleep for a few minutes, then glanced down at his clothes, soiled here and there with the remnants of Andrew's birth. Being a paramedic, the sight of blood and gore generally moved him not at all. Yet somehow, the recognition that this particular blood had once belonged to Katie did funny things to his insides. Usually, the blood Cooper washed off at the end of a run was the result of some violent act or tragic accident. Gunshot wounds, stabbings and vehicular or mechanical mishaps were the stuff of his everyday routine. And all too often, the victim he tried to save wound up dying instead.

But not this time. This time, instead of hearing a last gasp, Cooper had heard a first breath. This time, instead of feeling a body go limp and spiritless, the body he'd held in his arms had squirmed and fidgeted with vitality. This time, Cooper had experienced a profound joy at witnessing life instead of a helpless anger at witnessing another senseless, stupid death.

This time, for the first time, he had felt an odd, unnameable warmth surround his heart, had felt a tension unknot inside him that he'd never even realized he was carrying around. And for the life of him, he could understand none of it.

Pushing the strange workings of his mind away, Cooper returned to the kitchen, noting more thoroughly this time the sleek white design and numerous frivolous small appliances. The Brennans even had a huge, copper cappuccino maker that looked as if it had never been used. And he thought vaguely to himself that some people just had too much damned money. He headed for the sink, reached a hand behind himself to grab a fistful of his T-shirt, and pulled it over his head.

Contemplating the smudges of blood, he tossed the shirt into the trash can, then turned on the water to fill the sink. After dressing again in his relatively clean sweatshirt, he prowled around in search of Katie's bedroom. Surely, somewhere in the house, there was one of those inevitable bags packed in preparation for her trip to the hospital. People expecting their first kid always overdid things, packing months in advance for the hospital stay, and way too much stuff at that.

To his surprise, however, when he finally located the master bedroom, he found a huge suitcase on the floor, and scattered about it were far more articles of clothing and toiletries than were necessary for a brief hospital stay. Those items also seemed to have been heaved to the floor without care, as if Katie had been doing the packing when Andrew had decided to be born.

Cooper shrugged off the uneasy suspicion that wandered into his mind. Katie had told him her baby was coming three weeks before her due date, so she obviously hadn't anticipated his birth this morning. She couldn't have had a hospital stay in mind when she'd been packing yesterday. So why would she...?

He halted the question before his mind could form it. Her packing yesterday had no doubt been the result of something perfectly normal. Maybe she'd planned on joining her husband, wherever he was. Maybe she'd been going to visit a relative. Maybe she'd been stowing things in the suitcase to store them under the bed.

Maybe it was none of his business.

Definitely it was none of his business, Cooper corrected himself. Whatever Katie had going on in her life was completely immaterial to him. Last night, he'd been in the right place at the right time—as far as *she* was concerned anyway—and he'd been able to help her out in a very precarious situation. But once the ambulance arrived to ferry her and her son off to the hospital, it would put an end to any tie that might bind him to her. They were the proverbial ships in the night. The cliché of two strangers thrown together in a crisis. After this morning, Cooper would never see Katie Brennan again.

And why, in God's name, did that realization bother him so damned much?

Without even thinking about what he was doing, Cooper collected Katie's scattered belongings and arranged them as neatly as he could on the bed. Then he grabbed a few items that she would need for the hospital—functional, cotton, mommy-type underwear, a functional, cotton, mommy-type nightgown, functional, cotton, mommy-type socks and a few articles of clothing that would be big and loose enough to accommodate her still swollen abdomen. A perfunctory search of the closet netted him a modest-size Louis Vuitton overnight bag, and he filled it with Katie's things.

He tried not to think about the intimacy involved with what he was doing for her at the moment, just as he had tried all night not to think about the intimacy of experiencing with her the birth of her son. Inevitably, however, that intimacy never left the forefront of his brain for a moment.

He was a big boy, he reminded himself. He had seen women naked before, had shared things with some of them that went *way* beyond intimate. Katie Brennan was a virtual stranger. How could strangers be intimate?

"Jeez, Coop," he muttered to himself as he zipped the bag shut. "When did you become such a freakin' philosopher?"

He pushed away all the nagging, annoying questions that had been plaguing him since he'd entered the big town house, but couldn't chase them off completely. Demanding answers, they lingered in the corners of his mind, and he realized he'd probably never quite be able to dispel his memories of the one night he'd shared with Katie Brennan and her son.

Which was probably just as well, he decided further as he bolted from the bedroom. Because it was no doubt as close as he was ever going to come to being instrumental in the birth—or the life—of a child.

Three

Katie awoke to the sound of voices and realized she must have dozed off on the gurney as the orderly wheeled her to her room. When she opened her eyes, she saw Cooper Dugan, laughing in response to something a woman wearing raspberry-colored hospital scrubs was saying. Katie smiled, too, for a minute forgetting exactly who she was or what had happened to her. For one very brief, very magical moment, all she was aware of was her own existence in the same room with Cooper. And for that very brief, very magical moment, that was all that mattered in the world.

Then the baby in her arms snuggled closer to her, and she remembered that there was in fact something in the world infinitely more important than a laughing, handsome man. She bent her head to nuzzle her son's soft, downy black hair, and her smile deepened. She placed a kiss on the crown of his head and hugged him tight. The nurse and orderly helped her into her bed, and in the bright white light of the fluorescent bulb buzzing above her, she marveled again at Andrew—the new man in her life.

Men had come and gone in Katie's past, some leaving her with more than she'd had to begin with, some leaving her with nothing at all. But Andrew would be with her forever. And already, she could sense that the changes he wrought in her were, without question, changes for the better. Where before she had been wandering through life with absolutely no destination in mind, the birth of her son had endowed her with a sense of purpose, and a drive to make sure the two of them would never be torn apart.

It was almost terrifying, really, the genesis and immediacy of these new emotions inside her—this fear of harm coming to her child, this love that overwhelmed everything that had come before. She knew utterly and irretrievably that she would die before she would allow anyone—*anyone*—to hurt her son or take him from her. But instead of being frightened by such a certainty, she was oddly calmed by it. Motherhood was something that had always awed Katie in the past, when she'd observed other women participating in it. And now, finally, she understood why.

"Katie?"

Cooper's voice came to her softly from the other side of the room, and she lifted her head to find him slowly approaching. When he stopped beside her bed, he extended a hand to brush her hair back from her forehead. He completed the gesture with such familiarity, she doubted he even realized what he was doing. Then he dropped his hand to Andrew's head, cupping it softly over the baby's scalp before stroking his finger over one of the infant's pudgy cheeks.

"How are you two doing?" he asked quietly. "That wild ride in the ambulance didn't jar you too much, did it?"

She shook her head and whispered, "No," the single-word reply all she could manage for the moment.

"The nurse here..." He gestured over his shoulder toward the dark-haired woman in the hospital scrubs. "...she said she needs to check you and Andrew out. Think you're up to that?"

"Sure."

He straightened some, then hesitated for a moment, as if he didn't like what he was going to say next. "Um, listen, I'm really sorry, but I'm going to have to run out on you for a little while. There are still some snowbound people who need help, and I'm in a position to offer it."

"That's okay, Cooper," she said softly. "Hey, you did the important thing. You gave me my son."

He grinned at her, a crooked, very endearing grin that set Katie's heart to flip-flopping madly. "Yeah, well... I think you had more to do with that than I did."

"Maybe. Maybe not."

He covered her hand with his and squeezed hard for a minute before releasing it. "I'll come back tonight to see how you and the little guy are doing."

She nodded.

"Can I bring you anything? Make any calls for you?"

She knew he was referring to her husband, whom she had earlier assured him was always impossible to locate when he was traveling on business. She handled the question now as she had then, and simply repeated, "Thanks, but I can take care of that myself."

"If you're sure."

"I'm sure."

"Then I'll just bring you a strawberry milkshake, how's that?"

This time Katie was the one to grin. All night long, she had screamed out a number of insistent, often colorful, demands for a strawberry milkshake to help her through her labor. And as far as she was concerned, the idea still had merit.

"A strawberry milkshake sounds wonderful," she told him.

"You got it." He brushed an index finger tenderly over her cheek, an action so soft and quick, Katie almost thought she imagined it. Then he was gone, and she watched as the door swung closed silently behind him, and wondered why she was going to miss him so much once he was gone from her life.

"This won't take long."

The nurse's voice brought Katie's attention around. Reluctantly, she surrendered Andrew, and watched closely as the other woman swaddled her son in a flannel blanket and settled him in a clear, plastic bassinet.

Then she turned back to Katie and said, "We're going to have to take Andrew to the nursery for a little while for—"

"No."

The quietly uttered objection stopped the nurse short. "What?"

"You can't take Andrew anywhere. He's staying here with me."

"But—"

"He's staying here with me."

There must have been more fortitude in her voice than she thought she had been able to manage, because the nurse nodded once and said, "Okay. I'll have the neonatologist come examine Andrew here."

"Thank you."

"Now, let's see about your blood pressure."

Obediently, Katie extended her arm, then remained silent for the rest of her exam. The neonatologist came to look over and measure Andrew, deeming him fit and hearty and perfectly capable of facing up to life. When it was all over, the nurse presented Katie with a sheaf of papers in a rainbow of pastel colors. Most of them simply required her signature. But one of them—the one she had known was coming but dreaded nonetheless—required information for Andrew's birth certificate.

Automatically, she filled in the blanks that requested the pertinent information about herself, but she hesitated when she came to the line that asked, *Father's name.* She wondered helplessly how she could avoid identifying William as Andrew's father, wondered, too, what would happen if she just left the line blank or filled it in with the word *unknown.* Would William still have a strong case for taking Andrew away from her if she failed to identify him as the baby's father? Would the act of identifying no one at all—thereby making herself sound promiscuous enough that she didn't even know who had fathered her child—make it easier for William still?

Katie was still pondering her dilemma when, as if prompted by providence, the nurse in the raspberry-colored scrubs said the magic words for her.

"That husband of yours is quite a guy."

Katie's head snapped up, and she stared at the other woman. "What?"

The nurse stared back. "That guy who came in with you," she said with an indulgent smile. "You know...your husband. I mean, I only got to talk to him for a minute, but he seems like a great guy. He's been so attentive since you arrived, fussing over you like a mother hen, ordering everyone in the hospital around like a general. He obviously loves you and the baby very much."

"But Cooper's not...he and I aren't married."

The nurse nodded knowingly. "Well, maybe the birth of his son will bring him around. Men usually start to settle down when they have a child to think about. I'll bet the two of you tie the knot before long."

"But..."

Katie wasn't able to complete her objection, because an idea exploded in her brain when she understood the other woman's misconception. It was an idea she really had no business entertaining. An idea she tried to squash the second it fired to life. Really, she did. Because the idea she had was unthinkable. Reprehensible. Immoral. What she had in mind was no way to repay all the kindness and patience Cooper had shown to her and her son. He may very well have saved both their lives last night. There was no way she could allow these people think the two of them were romantically linked.

There was no way she could inscribe his name on the line where the birth certificate application asked for the name of Andrew's father.

But as if they had a mind of their own, Katie's fingers gripped more tightly the pen in her hand, and she watched with an almost detached fascination as they wrote out, in big, block letters, COOPER DUGAN. The next lines, however, stopped her short. *Father's Social Security number. Father's age. Father's place of birth.*

Okay, she could probably guesstimate Cooper's age to be late thirties. And, considering his accent and the manner in which he spoke, she thought it might be reasonable to assume he had been born in the area—the area being either Pennsylvania, New Jersey or Delaware, which at least narrowed the search to three states. Probably. But Social Security number? That was a tough one.

"Um," she began when she realized the nurse was waiting for her to finish completing the documents, "I can't seem to remember...uh...Cooper's Social Security number right now. Is it okay if I finish filling this out when he comes back?"

The nurse shrugged. "Sure. No problem. Just as long as we have it before you check out."

"Okay. I promise."

The nurse turned to leave, calling over her shoulder as she went, "Ring if you need anything."

"I will. Thanks."

The moment the door swung closed behind the nurse, Katie's mind lurched into action. She had to get out of here, she thought frantically. As soon as she could do so without raising too much suspicion. Never mind that she was still exhausted from the birthing experience. Never mind that she was still in pain. Never mind that she had just done something heinous to a perfectly nice man, making him legally responsible for a child that wasn't his.

Never mind that the act of fleeing would ensure that she never saw Cooper Dugan again. At least in disappearing, he'd know she had no intention of forcing him to acknowledge that fake responsibility.

None of that mattered. Only Andrew mattered. Whatever she had to do to keep him safe, to keep him with her, Katie would do it. She could not—would not—lose her son. She could give up anything else. But not him. Never him.

Someday, somehow, she hoped Cooper would understand what had driven her to do what she'd done. Someday, somehow, she hoped she and Andrew would be in a position to explain. But until that day dawned, Katie had no choice but to disappear. It was the only way she could ever be certain that William wouldn't find her and take her son away.

Disappearing with Andrew, however risky, however chancy, however frightening, was the only alternative she had. It was for the best, she tried to assure herself further. All she needed was a little time to figure out what she was going to do. Everything, eventually, would work out just fine. Unfortunately, she knew assurance would be a long time in coming.

"Oh, Mr. Dugan!"

Cooper spun around quickly at the summons, sending the balloons he clutched in one hand bouncing into a frenzy of colliding color, and causing him to release completely the huge, stuffed bear he'd held in the other. Only through some fast dancing and shuffling did he manage to save the bouquet of red roses he also had tucked under one arm, and the strawberry milkshake he balanced along with the balloons.

He didn't react in such a way because he thought someone was calling out to *him*—no one ever referred to him as *Mr. Dugan*—but because that tiny little part of Cooper that would remain a frightened child forever feared his father had risen from the grave, and was barreling down the hospital corridor toward him, brandishing his belt with the big, gold buckle gleaming.

Naturally, Cooper remembered almost immediately that his father was nowhere around. Nearly fifteen years had passed since Mike Dugan's death, even more time than that since Cooper had last run out on the sonofabitch, shocked by the blood on his own knuckles after he'd broken the old man's nose. No, it was the nurse Cooper had met earlier who approached him now, the one who had been seeing to Katie. With a shuddering sigh, he swallowed his terror whole, and forced himself to breathe as normally as he could.

"Yeah?" he said when the nurse was beside him. He congratulated himself for the steady timbre of his voice.

"Mr. Dugan, I need your Social Security number."

Still a bit shaken, Cooper recited the numbers from memory without questioning the woman's request.

"Date of birth?" she asked.

Again, he surrendered the information automatically.

"Place of birth?"

"Gloucester City, New Jersey," he told her.

Suddenly, it dawned on him that he was offering snippets of his personal life to someone whose name he didn't even know, and revealing them for no reason he could fathom. He also noted belatedly that the nurse was writing the information down.

"What's going on?" he asked her as he bent to retrieve the wayward teddy bear. He straightened, and as he rearranged his loot, asked further, "Why do you need all that information?"

The nurse, still scribbling away, replied without looking up. "We need it for your son's birth certificate."

Certain he'd misunderstood, he sputtered, "You . . . you need it for *what?*"

Finally, the nurse looked up from her clipboard, her expression bland. "Your son's birth certificate," she repeated. "Your . . . um . . . your girlfriend left without completing the form."

Cooper shook his head hard, trying to wake himself from what could only be a bizarre dream. "My son . . . ?" he repeated quietly, the words feeling more than a little strange on his tongue. "My girlfriend . . . ?" he added in the same tone of voice. Then the rest of the nurse's statement hit him. "She *left?* Katie's gone? Where? What the hell is going on here? She just had a baby. How could she leave?"

The nurse stared at him as if he were something she'd normally vacuum up from the carpet. She pulled her clipboard toward her, and crossed her arms over it and her chest. Then she cocked one dark eyebrow at him, and he knew he wasn't going to like one bit whatever she was going to tell him.

"Ms. Brennan checked herself out of the hospital this morning. If you had been here to meet her like you were supposed to, you would have realized that."

Cooper had intended to be there earlier this morning. Not because he'd thought Katie was going to be leaving, but because he'd wanted to check on her and Andrew and make sure they were okay. Actually, he'd planned to return the night before, but he'd wound up making runs until nearly midnight. By then, hospital visiting hours were over. So he'd waited until this morning to come by. Hey, he'd needed the sleep anyway. And judging by the strange reality to which he'd awakened, he obviously still hadn't gotten enough.

"Let's start all over here, okay?" he asked hopefully.

The nurse opened her mouth to say something, but he lifted a hand, palm out, to stop her.

"Yesterday," he said, "right around lunchtime, I arrived at this hospital in an ambulance with a woman who had just delivered a baby. Am I right about that?"

The nurse nodded. "Of course. You—"

He held up his hand again, and the nurse bit off whatever she had been about to say. "And the woman's name was...?" he asked, letting the question trail off so that the nurse would answer it for him.

She pulled her clipboard away from her chest and glanced at it only slightly before telling him, "Katie Brennan."

He released a sigh of relief. "That's right. Katie Brennan. And her son's name?"

The nurse studied the clipboard again. "Andrew Cooper Brennan Dugan."

Cooper nodded his head as she revealed the first three names, then quickly switched to shaking it at her recitation of the last. "No, that's not right. It's Andrew Cooper *Brennan*. Period. No Dugan. His name ends at Brennan. Right?"

The nurse turned her clipboard so that Cooper could view it. "No, she said she wanted to have both her last name *and* yours as part of the baby's legal name. So it's Andrew Cooper Brennan Dugan. Says so right here on the birth certificate application. Ms. Brennan did get that much filled out, anyway."

"Let me see that." The request was just a formality, as Cooper had already snatched the clipboard from the nurse's hand.

"Hey!" she objected.

But he ignored her. For there, enhanced with Katie's delicate, scrawling signature, were the documents in question, filled out exactly as the nurse had told him they were. Katie had named Cooper as Andrew's father on the birth certificate application. In black and white and triplicate. For all the world to see. She had made her son his son, too. In the eyes of the law and the Commonwealth of Pennsylvania, anyway.

"This doesn't make any sense," he muttered. "Why would she do something like this?"

"Check out early?" the nurse asked, obviously misunderstanding the question. "Because she has no insurance, that's why. I mean, your policy will cover the nursery charges, of course, because the baby is your dependent. But since you haven't *married the baby's mother*," she added, placing emphasis on the last part of her statement clearly to indicate her disapproval of Cooper's moral misconduct, "the bills for her portion of the hospital stay will have to be out-of-pocket. So she checked out early to save you both some money."

"No, I mean—"

"Naturally, she didn't want to leave without the baby, so she checked him out, too," the nurse continued, ignoring Cooper's interjection. "Since you didn't show up to meet her this morning, she took a cab home. And frankly, Mr. Dugan," she added, "I thought better of you than to do something like that."

"But..." Cooper's voice trailed off again, before he completed his statement. His head was buzzing with confusion, and all he could do was stare at the hospital chart in his hands.

"Your girlfriend was all ready to go when I went in this morning," the nurse continued. "Her doctor wanted her to stay longer, but since there were no complications with the delivery, and since she and the baby were perfectly healthy, and since it's not at all unusual to be released so quickly, nobody had a problem with letting her go."

"But...but...but what about me?" Cooper finally asked, his mind still reeling as it tried to process so much misinformation. "I might have had a problem with it."

The nurse snatched back her clipboard. "Then you should have been here this morning when your girlfriend was ready to leave."

"But—"

"Now if you'll excuse me, I have to go file these forms."

"But—"

"Go home to be with your new son, Mr. Dugan," the nurse told him as she sifted through the collection of forms. "And not that it's any of my business, but you might want to think about marrying that woman. Make yourself a proper family. Do the right thing."

With that, Cooper found himself alone, without the nurse in the raspberry-colored scrubs who had become the booming voice of moral integrity. And even though he had done nothing wrong where Katie and her son were concerned, even though Katie was the one who had overstepped the boundaries of reason and propriety, Cooper felt guilty and duly taken to task. Why? He couldn't begin to imagine. But for some reason, he suddenly felt as if he were the one who needed to set things to right.

For some reason, he suddenly felt like he really should do the right thing and marry Katie, thus making his son legitimate. Thus making the three of them, as the nurse had said, "a proper family." Even though Katie was still a virtual stranger. Even though Andrew was in no way his son.

The only problem was, Cooper had no idea where the other members of his newly formed family could be.

Four

Normally, Cooper couldn't get out of the supermarket fast enough. Normally, he stood in the check-out line shifting his weight restlessly from one foot to the other, and shaking his head in amazement at the headlines that screamed out from the tabloid racks about alien Elvises, mutant gerbil children and man-eating dieffenbachias. Normally, all he wanted was to escape the legions of slow-moving blue-haired ladies, screeching, whiny toddlers and single guys like himself who knew of no other aisle outside the frozen food section.

But he hadn't been feeling normal for some time now, and today he didn't mind lingering behind the woman ahead of him in line. And not because of her cascade of blond hair or the slim, tanned legs extending from her tight cut-offs, either, although he had noted those things about her right off. What held Cooper's attention now was the woman's baby.

He had no idea how to gauge the age of the infant strapped into the carrier that had been settled in the seat part of the grocery cart ahead of him. Nor did he have a clue as to the baby's gender. It could be a two-week-old boy or a seven-month-old girl for all he knew about babies. Hell, before today, the only time he'd been this close to one had been the night he'd delivered—

But he wouldn't think about that. He wouldn't think about Katie and Andrew Brennan and the fact that the two of them still haunted his dreams nearly two months after he'd last seen them. He wouldn't think about how he'd gone back to Katie's house in Chestnut Hill—at least, what he'd *thought* was Katie's house in Chestnut Hill—only to find it inhabited by an elderly couple who'd called the place home since 1958, and who had never heard of any family in the neighborhood named Brennan.

He wouldn't think about the fact that there were no Brennans in the Philadelphia phone book that had a Chestnut Hill address. Nor would he wonder yet again why Katie had given the hospital a phony Las Vegas address as her own. God knows he wouldn't recall yet again his concern about being named Andrew's father on the baby's birth certificate. And he wouldn't think about the fact that he had absolutely no hope of ever finding Katie or Andrew again to demand answers for all the questions that would trouble him for some time to come.

Instead, Cooper focused again on the baby in the grocery cart, who stared back at him with a steady, unblinking gaze, eyes huge and brown and mesmerizing. Then the baby smiled, a wide, toothless grin that crinkled its eyes at the corners and wrinkled its little nose, and it stuck its tongue out at Cooper and uttered a heartfelt, and very wet, "Spthibble."

The baby's unabashed commentary made Cooper laugh. He hadn't even realized he'd reacted in such a way until the leggy blonde turned around and began to laugh, too.

"He likes you," she said. "He doesn't usually smile that way at strangers."

Cooper glanced up long enough to acknowledge her comment, then looked back down at the baby. "It's a boy, huh?"

The woman nodded. "As of the last time I changed his diaper, anyway."

Cooper smiled. "How old?"

"He'll be five months next week."

"Cute kid."

"Yeah, I think so, too."

"Is he a lot of trouble?"

The woman chuckled. "Oh, yeah. The whole time I was pregnant, all of our friends with kids kept saying, 'You can't imagine how much your life will change once you have that baby.' And my husband and I kept saying, 'Yeah, yeah, we know. We're ready for it.'" Her chuckle turned to laughter. "We had no idea. You really can't imagine what a huge life change it is until you have one of your own."

This time Cooper was the one to nod.

"But he's worth it," the woman said as she stroked her son's cheek. Her voice oozed affection, and her eyes shone with happiness. "He's just so wonderful. You can't imagine that part, either, until you have one of your own."

"Yeah, maybe..."

His voice trailed off, leaving unfinished whatever he'd intended to say. The cashier barked out a total to the woman in front of him, and he watched as she wrote her check, picked up her purse and began to roll her cart away. Seemingly as an afterthought, she turned around to Cooper again.

"Thinking of having one of your own?" she asked with a smile.

He shook his head resolutely. "Nope. Just curious."

She laughed again. "Better watch yourself. That's what *I* used to say." And with that, she turned around again and exited the supermarket.

Cooper watched her go, finding some solace in the fact that a person could have a child and still be interesting, attractive and happy, not to mention maintain a sense of humor. For some reason, he'd thought all that would dry up once a person became a parent. Wasn't that how it usually worked? You had a kid, you bought a house in the 'burbs, and you started worrying about aphids and driving a minivan. You picked up weight and lost your hair, and you started saying things like, "Turn that music down" or "When *I* was your age" or "Finish your broccoli—children are starving in Europe."

Yet there went a woman who, if she hadn't been married, he probably would have asked out. She didn't seem like a mom. She seemed like . . . fun. She was even kind of sexy. Go figure. Who knew?

It was a thought that came back to taunt him that evening when he answered the knock at his front door and opened it to find Katie Brennan standing on the other side.

Just like that.

For a moment, he could only stare at her, half convinced she was nothing more than a mirage, a simple refraction of light resulting from the bloodred sun that hung low in the sky behind her. Immediately, however, he realized she was not. Because if she was a mirage, he would be seeing her as he had the last time, and this Katie was entirely different from the one he had met two months ago.

For one thing, she was much thinner—too thin, really. And her hair was a bit longer, though it lacked the luster and softness that had been present before. Her face was paler now than it had been even in childbirth, the skin drawn tightly over high cheekbones and a narrow nose. And dark circles stained the undersides of her eyes, making them appear even larger and a stormier gray than they had before.

She looked more exhausted than she had the last time he'd seen her. More fragile. More frantic. And Cooper could scarcely believe his good fortune that she had come back to him.

For one long moment, he could only stand stock-still staring at her. Then a baby's soft cooing punctured the silence, and Cooper dropped his gaze to the infant she clutched in her arms. Where Katie seemed to have deteriorated into almost nothing, Andrew was fat and pink and thriving. It was as if the baby had taken his vitality from Katie, as if she had literally given of herself to keep him hale. He gazed up at Cooper with a bland expression in his blue-gray eyes, then turned his attention back to his mother. Cooper didn't know much about babies, but he could have sworn Andrew looked worried about his mom.

"Help me."

They were the first words Katie had spoken to Cooper so long ago, on a cold, snowy night when her child's welfare had so clearly superseded her own. Now it was springtime, a bright, balmy evening full of promise, and she repeated the words again with exactly the same intonation. She was asking for help for herself, but she was obviously demanding it for her son.

"Katie . . ." Cooper began.

But words beyond that failed him. What could he say? What did a man say to a woman with whom he'd spent a solitary night, a night when he had shared with her the birth of her child? What did a man say to a woman who had named him as that father's child, despite the fact that he was a complete stranger? To a woman who had then disappeared without a trace? A woman who had haunted his dreams virtually every night since? Who had completely turned his life upside down and caused him to reevaluate everything he'd once held as truth?

Just what was a man supposed to say in a situation like this?

"Cooper, please," Katie said, sparing him from having to utter something himself. "You've got to help me. Help us. Andy and I . . ." She sighed fitfully and bent to retrieve a battered duffel bag at her feet. Then, without waiting for an invitation, she pushed past him into the apartment. "We're in trouble," she concluded. "Big trouble. You've got to help us."

Still stunned by the turn of events, Cooper mentally flicked the automatic pilot button in his brain to the On position. He closed his front door without slamming it at all, turned to look at Katie again and said, "Gee, long time, no see. How've you been, Katie? What's new?"

She gaped at him for a moment. "I . . . Cooper . . . Andy and I . . . We . . ."

This time words seemed to fail Katie. She dropped the duffel bag onto the floor again and shifted her weight from one foot to the other, repositioning the baby so that his head rested against her shoulder. Cooper took a few steps toward her before he even realized he was moving, then stopped.

"Oh, gee, where are my manners?" he said, smacking his palm to his forehead with much vigor. "Can I offer you something? Coffee? Soda? Child support?"

She sighed again and raised her hand, rubbing fretfully at her jaw before resting it over her eyes. "You're talking about Andy's birth certificate, aren't you? Look, I can explain that."

He emitted a chuckle, but there was absolutely no humor in the sound. "Oh, I certainly hope so. It's not every day a man becomes a father. Especially after a one-night stand with the baby's mother that involved delivering the child instead of actually conceiving it."

"Cooper, you don't understand—"

"That's right, I don't. And you said you could explain, so . . ." When she made no move to offer the promised explanation, he added, "I'm waiting."

But Katie only continued to stare at him in silence. Finally, she said, "Do you mind if I sit down? I'm really tired."

He gestured toward the sofa expansively. "By all means. Do make yourself at home. You are, after all, the mother of my child."

She shook her head at him mutely, but instead of seating herself on the couch, she bent to open her duffel bag. After withdrawing a brightly colored quilt, she spread it haphazardly on the carpet and lay Andy carefully down upon it, belly to the floor. Then she scattered a few toys within reach, and sat cross-legged on the rug beside him, absently stroking her palm across his back. But still, she said nothing.

Cooper moved to a chair across from her to observe the byplay between mother and child, and continued to be mystified by the turn of events. Katie traced her fingers slowly up Andy's spine, then opened her palm over the small of his back and left it there. Somehow, she seemed to be drawing strength from her son, when clearly the opposite had been true for the last two months. She kept her head bent toward the baby, her dark hair falling over the side of her face so that Cooper couldn't make out her expression. When she finally lifted a hand to push her hair behind her ear, he saw that she was silently crying.

Something inside him that had been wound tight slowly began to unravel. "Katie," he finally said softly, "what are you doing here?"

When she glanced up, her expression was startled, as if she had forgotten where she was and whom she was with. Hastily, she brushed the dampness from her cheeks and straightened.

"I've been trying to get to you for about a week now," she said, her voice sounding a little rough and ragged. "I couldn't do this by myself anymore."

"Do what?"

Instead of replying to his question, she looked down at the baby again and continued, "I had to find someone I could trust. But there is no one. At least, I didn't think there was. Then I thought of you. I figured I could trust you, that you'd be willing to help me and Andy."

Cooper's gaze dropped to her left hand, flattened palm down against the floor. Her wedding ring was still firmly in place, the cache of diamonds catching the early evening sunlight that tumbled through the window in a haze of reddish gold, reflecting it back in a dozen shades of copper and blue.

"What about your husband?" he asked. "Shouldn't he be the one you turn to in times of trouble? Can't he help you?"

Katie's head snapped up again, and for the briefest of moments, something hard and gritty shone in her eyes. Then the flicker of whatever it was vanished, and Cooper decided he must have been seeing things, a trick played by the fickle light of the setting sun.

"No," she replied quietly. "He can't." But she said nothing more to elaborate.

Cooper inhaled slowly and released the breath in a soft whistle of disquiet. "Why not? Where is he?"

The last thing Katie wanted to do was reveal to Cooper what an idiot she'd been where William was concerned. There was also the small matter that, in spite of coming to him for help, she really wasn't altogether certain she could trust Cooper completely. After the last two months she'd spent on the run, she'd learned that it wasn't possible to be too paranoid when people were out to get you.

For all she knew now, Cooper was on William's payroll, too. After all, he'd been Mr. Johnny-on-the-spot when it was time for her to have her baby, hadn't he? *She'd* certainly never called anyone to come help her out, had she? But there he'd been, just in the nick of time to help her have her baby. How did she know he hadn't telephoned William as soon as he'd left her in the hospital, to let her bogus husband know she was safely ensconced in the maternity ward at St. Teresa's, just ripe for the picking as soon as the snow melted enough for William to get through?

Although Katie still didn't have anywhere else to turn, and although she felt in her heart of hearts that the man before her was more than worthy of her trust—at least, her gut instinct led her to be *pretty* sure he was, anyway—she decided it might not be a bad idea to watch her back where Cooper Dugan was concerned, just in case.

Of course, that still didn't give him the answer he was waiting for, she reminded herself, the one concerning her husband's whereabouts. So she simply blurted out the first thing that popped into her head.

"Tahiti," she said quickly. "He's in Tahiti. On business. Long, long business. He's been there for weeks and won't be back until the end of the month. So you're the only one I can trust for the time being."

"Riiiiight," Cooper muttered. "Tahiti. Of course. And your house in Chestnut Hill. Why is it that I couldn't find a listing in the Philadelphia phone book for any Brennans with your street address?"

"Because we're unlisted."

At least that much was true, Katie thought. She'd always known William was a real privacy freak, but it wasn't something that had ever much bothered her. She'd just assumed it was because he was rich and held a prominent position in a well-known chemical manufacturing corporation. She'd thought his desire to maintain their privacy had been to protect her. She hadn't realized it was because he was a bigamist leading a double life.

Cooper nodded indulgently. "I see."

What Katie could see was that he didn't believe her for a moment, but right now that was the least of her worries. "Look," she tried again, "will you help me out or not?"

"Maybe you should start over," he suggested. "At the beginning."

She nodded. "I probably should." Her gaze met his levelly again. "But I won't. I'll start at the end. The night you first came to my house."

To Cooper, that actually was the beginning, but he wasn't about to argue semantics with Katie now. Not when she was about to start answering all those questions that had been bothering him for months.

"I was packing to leave my husband when my water broke," she began, holding up a hand when he opened his mouth to ask her why. "Never mind why," she told him, reading his thoughts. "It's too complicated for me to even try to explain. Just...I had to get out of there. Unfortunately, Andy decided to come early, and that changed my plans."

Cooper's gaze dropped to the baby lying in the middle of his living room floor. Andy had fallen asleep, one tiny fist doubled up near his head, his mouth pursed in a minuscule O. His eyelashes were dark and thick, sweeping down on his cheeks like fine, sooty feathers. The black curls that had been so thick on his head when he was born seemed to be thinning in places. But overall, the baby appeared to be twice the size Cooper remembered him being. Andy slept so peacefully oblivious to the turmoil that was obviously tearing his mother apart. It was the sleep of the innocent, the untroubled. Cooper wished he could sleep that soundly at night himself.

"Then you showed up," Katie continued, her eyes locking with his again. "Out of nowhere. You were like this big, blond, shining knight that came out of the snow to make everything better that night, Cooper. I don't know if it was the fear of impending birth, or overactive hormones making me hallucinate or what, but..."

She laughed, the first even vaguely happy sound he'd heard her make since she'd arrived at his front door. Unable to help himself, he smiled in response.

"But it was like you were my savior that night. Like your showing up was meant to be—I think you yourself called it destiny. I can't think of any other way to explain it. I was scared and on the verge of panic, but you appeared out of the storm to make me feel safe. You made me feel like as long as you were there, everything would be okay."

She dropped her head again when she continued, "I wasn't thinking straight when I filled out the application for Andy's birth certificate, but I think that's why I fingered you as his father. Andy's real father...my...my husband..."

She sighed, raked an unsteady hand through her hair, then dropped it into her lap. But she said nothing more about Andy's real father.

Instead, she continued, "Your name on that piece of paper was like a talisman of some kind, a magic spell guaranteed to keep Andy safe, no matter what happened. I'm so sorry. I know I shouldn't have done it. I was half out of my mind when I did. I know it's unforgivable and probably illegal to boot. I wouldn't blame you if you called the cops right now." She looked up at him again. "But I don't think you will."

He shook his head. "No. I don't think that's necessary. But I still don't understand any of this. I still don't understand why you named me as Andy's father instead of your husband. It doesn't make sense, Katie."

"I know. And now that I try to explain it, I'm not sure I can. I just...I panicked at the hospital, Cooper. William and I had been having problems, and..." Another fitful sigh, another nervous drag of fingers through her hair. "I was exhausted and frightened and confused. But as crazy as it sounds, I did what I did because I cared about you. And because I knew you cared about me and Andy."

"You're right. That does sound crazy."

But what was *really* crazy, Cooper thought, was his realization that he was more focused on her confession that she cared for him than the fact that she'd made him legally responsible for a child that belonged to another man.

She was a married woman, he reminded himself. Even if she had been packing to leave her husband, she still wore the ring that symbolized her union with that other man. Whatever had gone wrong in her marriage might still be wrong, but it might go right again any minute.

Cooper couldn't afford to care that Katie cared for him. Her life was obviously a mess right now, and she'd dragged him into it with her. He should resent her. He should be angry with her. He should be calling a lawyer and suing her for something, and making damned sure she rectified her act of naming him as Andy's father.

Instead, he found himself wanting to reach out to her, both emotionally and physically. He wanted to take her in his arms and hold her close, then smooth back her hair and assure her that everything was going to be all right. Much to his dismay, Cooper realized he wanted to tell Katie she could stay with him for as long as she wanted, for as long as it took her to sort out her life and get on with it. But he knew that was the last thing he should do.

"You can stay here for as long as you want," he heard himself saying anyway. "For as long as it takes you to sort out your life and get on with it." With a dubious sigh, he added, "Regardless of when your husband gets home from... Tahiti."

Her expression when she met his gaze then was wary, but hopeful. "Do you mean that?"

Reluctantly, he nodded. "But you have to tell me what the hell is going on here, Katie. I'll help you as much as I can, but I can't help at all unless I have some vague idea what kind of trouble you're in."

"Andy and I just need a place to stay for a little while," she told him evasively. "Just until I can regroup and figure out what I'm going to do. We'll stay out of your way, I promise."

"Katie—"

"Do you mind if I lie down while he's asleep? A catnap would do wonders for me. Then I can tell you more."

He nodded again, even more reluctantly than before. He really wanted to hear more about this trouble she was in. But he also had to admit that she looked like hell. She was going to need a lot more than a catnap before she was close to regaining even a semblance of the woman she'd been.

Without another word, Katie stretched out on the floor beside her son, resting her head on one arm, draping the other protectively and possessively over Andy's back. Cooper opened his mouth to tell her she could at least move to the sofa, then closed it again. Somehow he knew she would insist on maintaining a physical connection to her son. For all he knew, she'd been sleeping on floors for the last two months, so comfortable with and resigned to the position did she appear. In seconds, she was fast asleep, her breathing deep and even and contented.

Cooper shook his head and called himself a fool. Then he went to his bedroom to straighten up and change the sheets on his bed. The least he could do was try to make Katie comfortable while she was staying with him. And Andy, too, he added belatedly. He may not know much about babies, but he liked to think he knew a little something about women. And women seemed to prefer things tidy. A little too tidy, in fact, which was why he always wound up avoiding too tight an entanglement with one.

His thoughts circled back to Katie Brennan and her son. *Tidy* was the last word he would use to describe his current relationship with them. But for some reason *entanglement* seemed way too appropriate somehow.

"You're a fool, Coop," he said under his breath as he put out fresh towels in the bathroom. "A first-class, certifiable, see-exhibit-A fool."

Yet the admonishment did nothing to make him change his mind.

Five

Katie awoke from sleep feeling unafraid for the first time in months, in spite of the fact that she couldn't quite remember where she was at first. Andy lay awake beside her, his head turned toward her, a soft smile playing about his lips. The two of them were on the floor of what appeared to be a living room, surrounded by bland furniture in muted earth tones, and no home accents to speak of. It was obviously a man's abode, a man who seemed to care little for creature comforts or touches of warmth.

Cooper.

His face roared up inside her head, and the sense of relief and well-being that accompanied the image made her smile. She and Andy were safe now. Cooper would make sure of that.

Katie had spent the last two months trying to find a suitable place for her and her son to hide. After leaving the hospital, she had returned with him to the Chestnut Hill town house long enough to pack a few things they would need. Then they'd headed straight for the bank—a suburban branch, not the one where Katie usually did business—and she had withdrawn nearly five thousand dollars from an account William had set up in her name for any incidental needs she might have.

She'd had no qualms about taking the money, and would in fact have withdrawn more if there had been any more in the account to take. She had a child to care for, after all, and whatever was necessary to be certain Andy had everything he needed, Katie would do in a heartbeat, without a second thought. It had taken her no time at all to realize that maternal instincts went well beyond nurturing and singing a child to sleep—they could be downright ruthless when the situation called for survival.

From the bank, she and Andy had proceeded to the bus station, where she'd paid cash for a ticket and where the two of them had boarded a Greyhound for Las Vegas. Somewhere in Colorado, however, Katie had decided that Las Vegas was too obvious a destination, that her friends there would be the first people William would turn to once he realized she was gone.

So she and her son had debarked in Durango and boarded another bus headed back to her hometown in Kentucky. But somewhere in Illinois, she'd decided Kentucky was too obvious, too. Anyway, she didn't know that many people back home anymore, and there were none she could fully trust. The people where she came from were poor and had few prospects, and William's money would inspire any of them to talk.

So Katie and Andy had boarded another bus back to Philadelphia. It was a big place, Katie had reasoned, and the only other place in the country with which she was familiar. It seemed like a good place to get lost in the crowd. And maybe, just maybe, she'd thought, William would never think to look for them right under his nose.

But the money she'd taken hadn't lasted long. She had scarcely a thousand dollars left, rolled tight into a cylinder at the bottom of her duffel bag. Also stowed at the bottom of her bag was some jewelry, a few nice pieces that William had given her, which, along with her wedding ring, she could gradually sell off when her money ran out.

But at some point on her journey, she'd realized that she and Andy needed something far more desperately than they did money. They needed help. They needed someone they could trust. Almost immediately, Katie had thought of Cooper Dugan. She had questioned scarcely a moment her decision that he was the one human being on earth on whom she could rely.

But because of the size of Philadelphia's metropolitan area, it had taken her a few days to locate him at an address in a Pennsauken, New Jersey. It had taken her a few days more to find Pennsauken. Once she had, however, she'd come right to his apartment.

Now that she was here, Katie felt herself relax for the first time since William's wife—his real wife—had knocked at her front door. But she was weak and exhausted and nearly at the end of her rope. Breastfeeding and caring for Andy had taken a physical and emotional toll on her she never could have imagined. She supposed the first few months after a baby's birth would be difficult in the best of situations. But when mother and child were both on the run, a viable existence became nearly impossible.

She glanced out the window, and was surprised to discover that it was dark outside. She wondered how long she had been asleep. Rubbing her eyes, she sat up and turned to stretch, and found Cooper standing in the doorway watching her.

He was wearing a paramedic's uniform of dark gray trousers and white shirt, with a badge and a patch that made him look very official and not a little intimidating. His pale blond hair shone almost white in the bright light behind

him, and for a brief moment, Katie was carried back to the
first night she'd met him. She hadn't been intimidated by
him then, either, she recalled. Instead, she'd been comforted by his appearance. Just as she was now.

"What time is it?" she asked him, trying to ignore the
funny little dance her stomach did at seeing him again.

"A little after nine," he replied softly.

She nodded. "Andy's going to be hungry again soon. I
better eat something before I feed him."

"I can fix you something. What would you like?"

She smiled her gratitude. "Anything is fine. Whatever
you've got."

"How about a sandwich? Baloney? Ham?"

"Ham's fine."

"Mustard or mayo?"

"Mustard."

"White or rye?"

"Rye."

He disappeared again, and Katie was struck by the normalcy and absolute boredom of the exchange they'd just
shared. She almost laughed out loud. She'd scarcely spoken to an adult in months, and now that she had the opportunity, the focus of the conversation was a sandwich. For
some reason, the knowledge delighted her.

Andy seemed perfectly content to wiggle around on his
quilt, so Katie moved to stand in the doorway between the
kitchen and living room, where she could keep an eye on
both men. Cooper's galley kitchen was no more decorated
or furnished than his living room was, lacking even a single
magnet fastening a note of reminder to the refrigerator door.
She shook her head. It was almost as if he feared that the
display of any minor detail would identify some aspect of his
personality he'd rather keep under wraps.

"I have to work tonight," he said as he slathered mustard on a slice of bread. "I don't always work nights—just
sometimes. I'm sorry, but I can't avoid it tonight."

She smiled. "That's all right, Cooper. You don't have to apologize. Of course you should go to work. I don't expect you to rearrange your life for me and Andy."

Without looking up, he replied, "Coulda fooled me."

Her smile fell. He was never going to forgive her for naming him as Andy's father on that stupid birth certificate. And she supposed she couldn't blame him for that. It had been a pretty awful thing to do to a perfectly nice man.

"I'll fix all that as soon as I can," she told him. "Whatever I have to do to correct it, I will. I promise."

He nodded, but said nothing more, just slapped a couple of slices of ham onto the bread, then shoved the concoction onto a paper plate beside a pile of potato chips.

"It's not much, but I don't eat at home that often," he offered in explanation as he scooted the plate down the counter toward her. "Sorry."

"Quit apologizing," she told him as she reached for the sandwich. "Are you kidding? This is better than most of what I've been eating for the last couple of months. Do you have any milk to wash it down?"

He poured her a glass, then stared at her in silence as she ate. Katie began to feel self-conscious, but refused to let it show. Instead, she did her best to pretend that there was absolutely nothing out of the ordinary about a woman having a baby and then immediately going on the run, only to turn up months later begging for help from a virtual stranger.

"Just where the hell *have* you been for the last couple of months?" he finally demanded. "I went back to your place in Chestnut Hill to look for you, but I got the wrong house. With all the snow and the confusion of that night, I couldn't remember the exact address. Needless to say, the house I thought was yours wasn't, and the people living there had never heard of you. And the Las Vegas address you gave the hospital didn't pan out. It was just something else that bothered me about your disappearance. A lot."

Katie took a bite of sandwich and chewed longer than was actually necessary, trying to stall. "Like I said, I wasn't thinking straight that day at the hospital. I gave them my last address in Las Vegas instead of mine and William's Chestnut Hill address, but I guess I got the numbers wrong or something."

She knew the explanation was every bit as lame as everything else she'd told him, but she could think of nothing better to say. With a single, covert glimpse of Cooper from the corner of her eye, she could see that he didn't believe her now any more than he had when she'd told him her husband was in Tahiti.

"So, where were you?" he asked.

"At home," she lied. "With my... with William. Trying to work things out. For a while, it looked like we were going to be able to deal with our problems, but, now..." She shrugged, at least able to manage some genuine confusion. "I don't know."

"Gee, that's funny," Cooper replied blandly. "I could almost swear you haven't been home since you and I left together for the hospital two months ago. A less trusting man than myself might think you're lying about that."

When she said nothing to counter his statement, he continued, "A less trusting man than myself might think you've been on the run for a while. Frankly, Katie, you don't much look like a woman who's been trying to fix her marriage. Frankly, Katie, you look like hell."

"Okay, I haven't been home for a while," she amended hastily. "Not since William left on business a few weeks ago. Lately, I've been on buses and in hotels, mostly." She paused long enough for another swallow of milk. "Like I told you, I've been trying to find a safe place with someone I can trust. But there is no one I can trust." She met his gaze levelly. "No one except you."

"I wish you'd stop saying that."

"Why?"

His lips thinned for a moment, and something not quite reassuring flashed in his eyes. "Because I'm not necessarily the trustworthy type, that's why."

"That's ridiculous, of course you—"

"Don't overestimate me, Katie."

The tone of his voice alarmed her. He'd bitten off the words as if they'd been painful for him to say. Not for the first time, she reviewed how little she did know about this man. She'd spent less than twenty-four hours in his presence the last time she'd been with him, and those hours had been consumed by extraordinary circumstance and accelerated emotion. Yes, Cooper Dugan had seemed like a nice man, and yes, he'd been her rescuer. But being a rescuer was his job. What did she really know about him as a person?

Not much, she conceded.

"Look, if you want me to leave," she began.

"No," he replied quickly. Quickly enough that it startled them both. "No, it's not that," he said more evenly. "Just... Don't expect too much of me, Katie, all right?"

"But—"

"I'll do my best to keep you and Andy out of harm's way, but..." He sighed, a tired, frustrated sound. "Just don't expect too much."

She nodded, not certain she trusted her voice to remain steady if she spoke.

"I have to go to work," he said quickly. "I changed the sheets on my bed for you, but I don't have a crib or anything for Andy."

"He can sleep in the bed with me," she told him, "or I can make a pallet for him on the floor."

She bit back her reaction that she should sleep on the couch instead, that there was no reason for Cooper to surrender his bed for her. Somehow, though, she didn't think it would sit well with him if she made the offer.

"Do you need anything for him from the store? Food? Diapers?"

She shook her head. "I'm breastfeeding him. And I have enough diapers for a couple of days. He'll be fine for now. We both will. Go to work."

He nodded, then pushed past her to leave, and if Katie hadn't known better, she would have sworn he positioned his body especially so that he could avoid coming into physical contact with her. But that was silly, she told herself. Why would he do something like that? Unless he just found her too repulsive for words and couldn't tolerate being any closer to her than he had to be.

"I'll be home before dawn," he called over his shoulder without looking back.

And with the slam of a door, he was gone. Katie watched him go, and wished she could feel a lot better about what she had gotten the two of them into.

It was still dark outside when Cooper got home. He stood in the doorway of his bedroom, looking at his own bed, completely unable to recognize it. At its center, bathed in his shadow, a dark-haired woman lay on her side, her arm circled protectively around a tiny baby clad in nothing but a diaper. Evidently having succumbed to the warm night in her sleep, she had kicked the sheet to the foot of the bed, and her T-shirt had ridden up over her cotton panties. In the darkness, Cooper could tell very little about how Katie looked half dressed. But he could imagine.

Boy, could he imagine.

No woman had ever slept in his bed before. Ever. Had sex there? Yes. Slept there? Never. That was getting too personal. Too intimate. Too close. Sleeping with someone involved a level of trust Cooper was unwilling—or perhaps even unable—to give. Yet he had offered his bed to Katie without a second thought. As if it were the most natural thing in the world to do. As if that were exactly where she belonged. Katie and her son. Just what the hell had he gotten himself into?

Ever since she'd shown up at his front door, he'd wanted to touch her. Some instinct inside him had commanded him to pull her close and keep her there and never let her go. He didn't know what made him react that way. Katie was no more beautiful or interesting or funny than any other woman he'd ever met. She was married to another man, for God's sake. She had a kid. She was in trouble. She was everything he should avoid in a woman. But none of that kept Cooper from wanting her. Badly.

She had haunted him since that night two months ago. Scarcely a day had passed that he hadn't wondered where she was, who she was with, whether she and her son were okay. He had assumed she'd gone back home to her husband, and that the two of them were basking in the glow of new parenthood. But after his earlier exchange with her, he could almost swear now that Katie hadn't seen her husband in months.

In spite of the odd things she'd said about the man after Andy's birth, in spite of her obvious fear and confusion, Cooper had assumed that Katie Brennan must surely have returned to the good life, to the man who loved her enough to make her his wife. Surely she must have worked out whatever marital problems she may have had. Surely she must have forgotten all about Cooper Dugan.

But now, he had no idea what to think. Now, the things she'd said that night, the way she'd seemed to feel ... Why did she need a place to stay? he wondered yet again. Who was she running from? Why was she in trouble? And dammit, why had she turned to him, instead of her husband, for help? Cooper shook his head, unable to understand any of it, certain he was being a fool to let her get to him this way.

He moved away from the door, pulling it closed softly behind him, even though he had found it open upon his return home. Katie trusted him, he reminded himself. Not only with her own welfare, but with her child's, as well. The realization stunned him. When he'd told her not to overestimate him, he'd meant it. When he'd told her he wasn't necessarily the trustworthy type, he'd meant that, too.

His life was as much a mess as hers was. He was just a little better about keeping that mess organized. Of course, he'd been doing it a lot longer than she had, too, ever since he was fifteen years old. Eventually, he supposed, Katie would get the hang of being alone and handling trouble. It just took a little practice was all.

Either that, he corrected himself, or she'd return home to a husband who would straighten it all out for her, a man who loved her enough to make sure she never got into trouble again. Unless, of course, it was her husband who was at the heart of this mess, a possibility Cooper couldn't ignore, because it was the one possibility that made the most sense.

A hopeful thread of something began to weave its way into his heart. Ruthlessly, he pushed it away. No matter what, Katie Brennan was a married woman. Even if her marriage wasn't ideal, it was still binding. Cooper in no way considered himself a moral man. But he wasn't about to go after someone else's wife.

Man, he hated working nights, he thought as he paced the length of the living room floor. It always wrecked the following day. He rubbed a knot at the base of his neck as he unbuttoned his shirt and shrugged out of it. His T-shirt came next, then he unbuckled his belt and unfastened his trousers, toeing off his shoes and kicking them aside. He was about to strip off the rest of his clothes to change into the ones he'd left for himself on the couch, when he heard a soft *click* behind him. He spun around to find Katie watching him, squinting in the light of the solitary lamp he had turned on.

Her T-shirt fell to midthigh now, but the knowledge of that was immaterial to Cooper. Because everything else about her was uncovered and revealed—her arms, her legs, her face, her eyes—and the absolute hunger with which she looked at him.

"Cooper?" she asked quietly before lifting her hands to rub the sleep from her eyes.

Or maybe she was trying to hide her eyes, he thought further, the idea poking his brain with a hazy, indistinct finger. Hiding her eyes to cover up her feelings. Or maybe in an effort to pretend she didn't see the longing inside of him, a longing he knew it was impossible for him to disguise.

He felt a part himself that had no business being active swell to life, and he immediately refastened his pants.

"You're up early," he muttered, hoping his voice didn't sound as gruff and anxious to her as it did to him.

She dropped her hands back to her sides, then immediately lifted them again, crossing her arms over her midsection. The gesture pushed her breasts up high, and Cooper fought back the thrill of awareness that rippled through him, forced himself to look at her face, her hair, the door behind her . . . anyplace but where his gaze wanted to settle.

"I heard you come in," she said quietly.

"Is Andy—"

"Still sleeping," she finished for him. "I piled some pillows around him, even though he's not even turning over yet. He'll be fine."

Cooper hesitated for a moment, feeling awkward and edgy. He found it impossible to take his eyes off Katie, even if he'd wanted to, which, of course, he didn't. Her dark hair was tousled from sleep, her eyes heavy-lidded, her skin a bit flushed. She looked warm and soft and inviting. She had just come from his bed.

And she was married to another man, he reminded himself viciously.

"And how about you?" he finally forced himself to ask. "Are you fine, too?"

She nodded. "That's the soundest sleep I've had in a while. It helped a lot."

He glanced away and mumbled something about coffee, then at her nod retreated to the kitchen with all the muster of a fleeing army. *She's married,* he chanted to himself with every step he took away from her. *Mar-ried, mar-ried, married, mar-ried...*

"How was work?"

The question came from the kitchen doorway, and Cooper spun around to find that Katie had followed him. In the brighter light of the kitchen, he could see her much better, could see that the circles under her eyes were a bit less severe, that some of the color had returned to her cheeks, that she seemed to be a bit more rested than she had been when she'd shown up at his front door twelve hours ago...

...and, beneath the thin fabric of her white, V-necked T-shirt, he could see the outline of two perfect breasts, swollen and heavy and crested by exquisite, dusky circles the size of silver dollars.

He closed his eyes and counted to ten and hoped like hell she couldn't see how hard he was.

"Cooper?"

"What?"

"How was work?"

"Fine."

"Are you okay?"

"Yes."

"You don't look okay."

"I'm okay."

"But—"

"I'm *okay.*"

"Okay."

When he opened his eyes, it was to discover much to his dismay that Katie was standing even closer now than she had been before. And Cooper's tiny kitchen gave a whole new definition to the word *close.* She stood leaning with her hip against the counter and one sock-clad foot settled on the other. Splashes of gold sparkled in her hair, and she smelled like his soap and his shampoo. He jerked the lid off a can of coffee and felt a good bit of the gritty grounds spill out over his hands.

"Dammit," he mumbled, reaching for the paper towels.

He stooped to sweep the coffee up dry, then Katie joined him on the floor with a wet rag, her efforts much more effective at cleaning up the mess than his own were. Her position allowed Cooper to look down the front of her shirt, something he most definitely never intended to do. It just sort of...happened. When she knelt in front of him, he automatically glanced up. But his gaze never got any farther than the neck of her nightshirt. Vaguely, he recalled reading or hearing somewhere about how women's breasts filled out during pregnancy and after childbirth. But he'd had no idea they would be so—

He was unable to complete the thought, because that was when Katie glanced up and caught him ogling her. Cooper felt her eyes on him, and he lifted his gaze to meet hers levelly. Her cheeks were flushed deep crimson, her pupils were dilated nearly to the edge of her irises, and her lips were slightly parted. Her chest rose and fell in rapid, ragged breaths. She looked like a woman on the verge of climax. And it was all Cooper could do not to reach out and pull her toward himself, and help her achieve that particular goal.

As she watched him watching her, it wasn't the first time Katie realized she'd made a mistake in coming to Cooper Dugan for help. The first time had actually been when he'd opened his front door, and she'd recognized right away that he was even more handsome than she'd remembered. Since that moment, there had been dozens of others when she called herself an idiot for ever thinking this situation could work.

Even after two months of not seeing him, she'd been unable to forget about Cooper Dugan. At least once every day she had wondered what he was doing, and who he was with. She had recalled how safe and contented he had made her feel during the short time he'd passed through her life. She remembered how gentle he'd been, and how quick to smile.

Only now, when it was far too late for her to do anything about it, did she realize that over the last two months, she'd halfway fallen in love with her memory of the guy. Why on earth had she thought it would be a good idea to turn to him for help?

Now, as she knelt on the kitchen floor, observing Cooper's reaction to her state of undress, she realized much to her horror that all she wanted to do was grab the hem of her nightshirt and pull it over her head. He was already half naked himself—a fact she found it impossible to over-look—so why shouldn't she be, too? In no time at all, the two of them could be panting and coupling like wild ani-mals, right there on the kitchen floor. Her eyelids fluttered down as a very graphic image of just such a union assailed her, a picture of herself bucking beneath Cooper as he drove himself deeply inside her, over and over and over again.

Immediately, her eyes snapped open, and she was re-lieved to discover that he had stood up. But that relief evaporated when she realized she was still kneeling before him, and that her position allowed her a rather gratuitous inspection of a part of Cooper she probably shouldn't be gratuitously inspecting. And she understood right away that he, too, had been entertaining thoughts along the same lines as her own. He was a tall, big-boned, broad-shouldered man, she reminded herself. She shouldn't be surprised that he was also so—

Oh, dear.

Hastily, she, too, stood, hurling the damp dishrag into the sink before turning away. She was about to bolt from the kitchen when the grip of firm fingers around her wrist stopped her. Without looking back, she tried to tug her hand free of his. But his long fingers only tightened around her, and he slowly pulled her back toward himself.

However, instead of wrapping his arms around her and covering her mouth with his—something she both wanted and feared at the same time—Cooper only pulled her flush against him. He tilted his head down and brushed his cheek against hers...once, twice, three times...until Katie felt her knees begin to buckle beneath her. He caught her capably, then dipped his head to her neck, and dragged his open mouth lightly down her throat and along her shoulder. So gentle was the caress, so warm was his breath against her skin, that Katie nearly moaned out loud at the feel of him against her.

Then, as quickly as he had embraced her, Cooper gently set her at arm's length.

"The only thing that's keeping me from taking you right here on the floor, right now," he said roughly, "is the fact that you're a married woman. And as long as you're living under my roof, Katie, it's going to have to be your job to remind me of that, because..."

He inhaled deeply, released the breath in a shuddering sigh, and with obvious reluctance, released her arms and dropped his hands back to his sides.

"Because...?" she encouraged him in a soft voice.

He swiped a hand fiercely over his face and pushed past her, but paused at the kitchen door, gripping the doorjamb with a white-knuckled ferocity. "Because I'm afraid that as long as you're living under my roof, your marital status is going to be something that just doesn't quite gel in my brain. I've done some dumb things where women are concerned. But I've never messed with another man's wife." He lifted his head to meet her gaze. "Not yet anyway."

With that, he shoved himself away from the door and into the living room. And it was all Katie could do not to shout out after him that she wasn't married to her husband at all.

Six

—

When Cooper awoke, it was to the sound of a woman singing. The tune wasn't one he recognized, so he kept his eyes closed for a moment, and turned his head to listen harder. The woman was singing about the man she loved. Something about how someday he'd come along. Something about how he'd be big and strong. And about how she'd do her best to make him stay. The woman singing was Katie. The song was melancholy. And she sang it as if she meant every word.

Cooper opened his eyes and stared at his living room ceiling and remembered that his life had been turned upside down. He rolled to his side and looked across the room, seeing his bedroom door open. Beyond it, Katie sat on the edge of his bed, rocking her body back and forth as she held her baby. She crooned to Andy softly, the way Cooper supposed mothers did sometimes, and somehow the sound of her voice calmed him, too.

Only then did it occur to him how quiet his apartment was. He had a stereo, a television, all the noisy gadgets that men—especially single men—usually collected. But he seldom took advantage of any of them. Simply because, more often than not, he spent his time anywhere but at home.

Home. Yeah, right, he thought. The word was meaningless to him. Home was some vague, hazy illusion kept alive by a bunch of die-hard political conservatives and bleeding-heart family organizations who just couldn't face up to the reality that The American Dream had turned out to be a nightmare.

No place like home? Cooper repeated the often-used phrase to himself with disgust. Hell, no place *was* home.

When he was a kid of barely fifteen, he'd performed an action that had been known back then as "running away from home." As if the building he had inhabited with his parents and sister had been a *home.* What a laugh. He'd preferred to think of "running away from home" as more accurately being "escaping another beating from his father by the skin of his teeth." It had been an act of survival, not rebellion, as the social workers had kept calling it. If he hadn't taken off, his father may well have beaten him to death one day.

So for once in his life, Cooper had gotten in the first punch, had popped his pop in the nose and broken it. The blood on his hand had shocked him. The expression on his old man's face had terrified him. He had turned and run from the house. Had run away. Had run for his life. And he had never gone back again.

Cooper hadn't been reunited with his family after that. He'd lived in a series of foster homes when he was good, on the streets or in youth detention centers when he was bad. At some point along the way, he'd realized his life was getting a little out of hand, going a bit beyond his control. So he'd turned to an old friend from the streets—really the only friend he'd ever had—who had studied to become a nurse and made something of her life.

Zoey had helped Cooper find his way to the medical field where he'd trained to become a paramedic. He'd started making a living doing something he enjoyed, had started making a difference in other people's lives by saving them. And he'd begun to feel as if there might be a halfway decent, halfway meaningful, human being dwelling within the fleshy shell that had carried him through life. Ultimately, he had even found a tenuous center inside himself to which he could cling in times of trouble.

That center eluded him now.

Because scarcely ten feet away, Katie Brennan was singing to her son about a man she wished she'd find. And all Cooper could do was lie on his couch wishing he was a man like the one she wanted, knowing instead that he would never come close.

He watched as she leaned over to place the sleeping infant in the middle of his bed, then position pillows around him should Andrew decide to move while he slumbered. She watched the baby sleep for a moment, as if needing to reassure herself that he would be all right. Then she tiptoed out of the bedroom, leaving the door slightly ajar, and silently approached Cooper.

He jackknifed up into a sitting position, then scrubbed both hands over his face and through his hair to rouse himself a little better. He'd changed from his uniform into well-worn jeans and a faded navy blue T-shirt, but was barefoot. Katie, too, had changed her clothes, he realized thankfully, and now wore a pair of baggy tan trousers and a very loose-fitting ivory tunic. He was relieved that her clothes were so nondescript and formless. Because he still couldn't quite dispel the image of that morning, of her bent over in front of him to offer a very substantial view of herself.

"That was nice," he said softly when she sat down beside him.

She glanced over at him, clearly confused. "What was?"

He tilted his head toward the bedroom door. "That song. The way you sang it. You have a good voice."

She smiled shyly and dropped her gaze to the floor. "Thanks. But it doesn't take much to make Gershwin sound good."

"You've still got a good voice."

"Thanks."

"Andy likes Gershwin, does he?"

She smiled and nodded. "It seems to work best when I'm trying to get him to go to sleep. Although he likes Sam Cooke and Cat Stevens, too."

Cooper chuckled. "Sounds like he's on his way to a pretty broad course of study in music appreciation."

Katie laughed, too. "Someday I'll introduce him to classical and jazz, but I'm going to need to find a home where I can put a stereo system first. Humming Mozart and Coltrane just isn't quite the same as hearing the original."

They simply sat for a moment, gazing at each other in silence, until Cooper managed to shake himself out of the pleasure he took in just looking at her. "What time is it?"

"About eleven-thirty."

He nodded. Five hours wasn't a lot of sleep, but it would do.

"There's coffee," she offered quietly. "Would you like some?"

"Please. Black."

She jumped up anxiously and retreated quickly to the kitchen. Her jerky motions and hasty disappearance told Cooper she was no more comfortable about the turn of events that morning than he was. It would probably be better for both of them if they just forgot about it. Funny thing was, though, he really had no desire to forget.

Katie returned with a cup of coffee, and he took it from her gratefully. After a few sips, he felt coherent enough to manage words of more than one syllable. In spite of that, what emerged when he opened his mouth was, "We still need to have that talk."

She nodded. "Okay."

He waited for her to continue, and when she didn't, wondered if he was the one who was supposed to talk next. Then, reassuring himself that yes, it was in fact Katie who owed an explanation, and not himself, he waited some more.

"Well?" he finally prodded.

She licked her lips and rubbed her hands nervously up and down her thighs. Cooper noted the action with interest, unable to prevent the curiosity that spiraled up in his brain. Just what did Katie feel like under those clothes?

She's married.

Damn the voice of reason, Cooper thought as he sipped his coffee again. "I'm waiting," he added when her silence dragged on longer.

"I know," she said quietly. "I owe you an explanation. And you deserve one, you really do."

He scrolled his free hand a few times, silently encouraging her to move the story along. "So, where is it?"

"Well, it's kind of tricky."

"So take your time. I don't have any plans for the day."

Katie drummed her fingers on her knees, and again, Cooper was fascinated by the small action. Her knees were probably beautiful, he thought. Slender and round and—

She's married.

And her calves, too, he thought further. They were doubtless perfectly formed, gently gliding curves of muscle that flexed and eased with every step she took. He had to bite back a wistful sigh. He always had been a leg man.

She's married. Although there was a lot to be said for breasts, too, of course. And he already knew Katie's were spectacular.

She's maaar-rieeed.

But what it all boiled down to, really, he knew, were the eyes. And Katie's eyes were filled with so many things. Sadness, humor, longing, intelligence . . . the knowledge of things Cooper himself would probably never experience.

She's married, you jerk. How many times do I have to say it?

Still trying to ignore the obnoxious little voice that had been haranguing him since Katie had arrived at his front door, Cooper gulped another swallow of coffee, grimaced as the hot liquid seared his tongue and throat, then told himself he deserved the pain for being such an ass.

"It's . . . it's my . . . my husband," Katie began, her voice stumbling over the announcement as she made it.

Right, Cooper remembered. Her husband. She was married. How could he have forgotten that?

"I've, um . . . I've sort of . . . that is . . . Well, I think you've probably pretty much guessed it for yourself already."

"Guessed what?"

"I, um . . . I suppose you could say I . . . I've run away from home," she continued.

Her choice of words made him slump back on the sofa and stare at her from beneath half-closed eyelids. "You've run away from home?"

Without looking at him, she nodded. "It's a long story."

"Like I said, I've got all day."

She lifted a hand and placed it lightly over her eyes. "I wish I could tell you that would be enough."

"What do you mean?"

She dropped her hand back to her lap and shook her head. "Nothing." She sighed heavily. "Look, I don't suppose you'd let me get away with just telling you that I'm having some marital difficulties and I need a place to stay while I sort them all out, and let it go at that, would you?''

Cooper thought about it for a minute. Marital difficulties. She had made him legally responsible for a child who actually belonged to her husband, and she was hiding out in his extremely no-frills apartment instead of returning to a gorgeous Chestnut Hill town house filled with every luxury a person could want. *And* if he wasn't mistaken—and he was pretty sure he wasn't—she had become prone to throwing looks his way that threatened to burn down the building. Yeah, that could qualify as marital difficulties, he conceded. But it explained nothing.

"Nope," he decided. "Not good enough. You promised me an explanation for your actions, not a description of your situation. I think I have a right to know why you gave me a child I never asked for, a child I don't want, a child I had no part in creating. Not to mention telling me why I should risk the wrath of your husband, should he discover somehow that you and I have been shacking up.''

Katie continued to stare at the carpet as she said, "I said you were Andy's father because I wanted him to have some kind of chance for a happy life. Because I don't want my...I don't want William to get his hands on my son.''

Vaguely, Cooper noted that she hadn't addressed the second part of his demand—the one about her husband—and was focusing, as always, on her son's needs instead. He told himself Katie and Andy weren't his problem. In spite of his epiphany the night the baby was born, in spite of the fact that since that night, Cooper had felt responsible for Katie and her son both, for no reason other than that he had been the one to witness and assist in the little guy's delivery, he told himself that Katie was on her own. If she had troubles, they were her troubles. It wasn't his problem.

He tried to keep his voice level and matter-of-fact as he told her, "I'd say Andy's custody is something you need to take up with your husband. Or else a good lawyer.''

"I can't afford one."

Cooper eyed the ring on her finger again, contemplating the continuous row of sparkling diamonds. He doubted very seriously that there was anything Katie couldn't afford. Nevertheless, he told her, "There's Legal Aid for people who can't pay for a lawyer. They can—"

"I'd need a really good lawyer for this," she interrupted him. "Legal Aid won't cut it."

"So hock the rock on your finger and hire a really good one," he said.

Katie lifted her left hand and inspected the ring that William had given her at their wedding in Las Vegas. It was beautiful, she had to admit, if much showier than the one she had picked out herself. The one she had chosen had been a wide gold band engraved with vines of ivy. William had assured her that diamonds were more her style. Laughing all the while behind her back, she was certain now. She had no idea how much the thing was actually worth. Several thousand dollars, certainly.

"It wouldn't be enough," she said softly. "There's not enough money in the world for me to keep that bastard at bay."

When she glanced over at Cooper, he was studying her from beneath heavy lids. It was impossible for her to tell what he was thinking. Doubtless he saw her as nothing more than a rich man's wife, one who was shallow and superficial and on the run because her husband didn't appreciate her, or because she was at the mercy of some bizarre, postpartum chemical reaction in her brain.

She really did want to tell him the truth. She really did want to give him the explanation he deserved. But she knew he wouldn't believe her once he had it. Why should he, when she could scarcely believe it herself?

"Will you throw me and Andy out if I go back on my word?" she asked him.

His eyes widened, and his eyebrows shot up in curiosity. "What?"

"If I refuse to give you that explanation I promised, will you throw me and Andy out on the street?"

"Of course not. But—"

"Then I'm going back on my word."

"Katie—"

"Just give me a week to figure things out, Cooper. Then I'll take Andy and get out of here. I'll see to it that his birth certificate is corrected. Then you'll never hear from me again."

"But—"

"One week," she repeated. "That's all I ask."

He sighed heavily, but his gaze never left hers. "How do I know that husband of yours isn't going to make trouble for me at some point in the future?"

"Because I'm going to make damned sure he never finds me."

"How do I know you'll leave in a week? What's to keep you from pulling this stunt again and telling me you need another week?"

Boy, he really did want to be rid of her, Katie thought. Then again, after what she'd put him through, she could hardly blame him for wanting to get this chapter of his life behind him once and for all.

"You have my word," she said softly.

"Oh, thank goodness for that." He twisted his lips into a sarcastic grin. "I'm sure your word is as good as gold."

She dropped her gaze back to the ring on her finger. "Yeah, Cooper, my word is," she told him. "You're just going to have to trust me on that."

Cooper gave her the week she requested, only to regret his decision within days of making it. Not only was sleeping on the sofa every night wreaking havoc on his back and in no way conducive to good sleep, but all too often, he awoke in the wee hours to hear Katie singing to her son as she fed him. The song was always something tender and sweet, and the sound of her voice was made all the more poignant because it came to Cooper out of the darkness, during that time of night when he felt most vulnerable.

Every morning, she made coffee and breakfast for him before he went to work, and every night dinner was waiting for him when he got home. She explained her actions by telling him she'd always loved cooking and hadn't had a chance to do much of it lately. She said it was the least she could do to repay him for his hospitality.

Hospitality, hell, he always thought when she said something like that. The last thing his feelings for Katie were was *hospitable*.

But what happened after dinner every night was what bothered Cooper most of all. Katie would spread Andy's quilt in the middle of the living room, the bright fabric providing the only splash of color in the otherwise pallid room—something that made it appear more than a little out of place. Then she would settle the baby on his belly at its center. She would smile and laugh at the child's antics—which, Cooper noted, mystified, consisted of little more than squirming and drooling—often scooping the infant up without warning to kiss his cheek and snuggle him close. Andy would respond with a soft coo and happy gurgle, a crooked, gummy smile playing about his tiny lips.

And inevitably, for some bizarre reason he could never begin to explain, Cooper would find himself responding to the scene. He would put down the newspaper he'd been peeking around to watch them, and move to the floor to join in the play. All the while, he would try to ignore the warm sensations that having Katie and Andy in his home made bubble to life inside him. All the while, he would remind himself that this was just a temporary arrangement, and that Katie belonged to another man, another life. All the while, he would tell himself not to let it get to him.

Even if things didn't work out for Katie with her husband—and increasingly, Cooper believed they would not—he reminded himself that she just wasn't the kind of woman he needed to get involved with. She needed a man who would stand by her. A man who would cherish her and see that she never wanted for anything at all. She was used to a kind of life-style Cooper could never afford to give her. He simply wasn't the man for Katie.

Or for Andy, either, he told himself on such a night. The baby and his mother had been resident in his apartment for four days, but Cooper felt no more comfortable about their invasion now than he had the Friday evening Katie had shown up at his front door. Actually, he had to amend as he stretched out on his side on the floor beside the baby, that wasn't exactly correct. He did feel comfortable around them. He just didn't feel comforted by the feelings the two of them were beginning to rouse in him.

The two of them evoked images in Cooper's brain that were completely foreign to him. Katie and Andy together were a family, ready-made. They were love. They were warmth. They were happiness. They were, in other words, an aberration. And he had no business thinking he had any place in their lives. He wasn't husband material by any stretch of the imagination. And he sure as hell wasn't fit to be anyone's father.

Whatever had stirred to life inside of him as a result of Katie's and Andy's visit was something he was certain would die the moment they left. Maybe sooner. This was just a new twist in an otherwise boring life, something to spark Cooper's imagination and make it work overtime for a while. Katie and Andy were a nice diversion. But they were just passing through his life on a trip to somewhere else. Hell, they'd literally shown up with luggage, after all.

But tonight, Cooper wasn't thinking about those things. Tonight, he was just enjoying their presence. He propped his elbow on the floor and leaned his head against his hand as he watched Andy wiggle around and try to reach for a rattle scarcely an inch away from his hand. After a number of trials and errors, the little guy managed to curl his fingers around the handle and jerk it toward himself. Inexplicably, Cooper felt a swell of pride wash over him when the baby achieved his goal, and he laughed out loud in triumph.

"All right, Andy," he said with a chuckle. "Way to go."

Katie laughed, too, and patted the baby on the back. "He's way ahead of most babies his age where small motor skills are concerned," she said proudly. "He'll be good with his hands someday."

Cooper nodded approvingly, even though it looked to him as if Andy's small motor skills still needed a lot of work before he was ready for paint brushes or power tools. "Maybe he'll be an artist when he grows up."

"Maybe. But I think he'll probably more likely be responsible for wiping out world hunger, curing every disease known to mankind, bringing peace to the entire planet and making the colonization of space a reality."

Again, Cooper nodded his agreement. "Yeah, you're probably right. But I'll bet he paints in his spare time."

Katie smiled. "That's my boy."

She, too, lay on the floor near the quilt, perpendicular to Cooper, with the crown of her head only inches from his. She rolled to her belly, flattened her palms on top of each other on the carpet, and rested her chin atop her hands.

"Did you always want to be a paramedic?" she asked out of the blue.

Cooper arched his brows in surprise and tilted his head back to look at her. "God, where did that come from?"

She shrugged. "I don't know. I just wondered. It's kind of an unusual occupation." She shrugged again, a little anxiously this time. "I was just curious. You don't have to tell me if you don't want to."

"No, it's not that."

"Then what?"

"Just—"

Her question was a perfectly innocent one, Cooper told himself, and had been asked with no ulterior motive other than the fact that Katie was curious about his line of work. It wasn't as if he were harboring government secrets or working on some hush-hush, scientific project. Why was he so reluctant to answer her?

He returned his gaze to the baby on the quilt, who was trying without much success to turn himself from his belly to his back. Without even realizing what he was doing, Cooper extended his hand toward Andy's, curling the infant's tiny fingers around one of his own. With some difficulty, the baby turned his head toward him and squeezed his newly discovered toy with much vigor. Cooper was surprised by the amount of strength in the action.

"No, I didn't always want to be a paramedic," he finally replied. But he said nothing more.

"When you were a kid, what did you want to be when you grew up?"

She wasn't going to let this go away unless he rudely refused to answer her, he thought. So, reluctant to spoil the quiet mood that had settled over them, yet knowing his response was going to do just that, he told her honestly, "When I was a kid, I just wanted to survive long enough to become an adult."

This time Katie was the one to arch her brows in surprise. "What?"

Cooper sighed in resignation. "For a while, when I was really young, I wanted to be a magician," he said by way of an explanation. "I wanted to be able to make myself disappear at will. Then I went through a phase where I wanted to be a truck driver, so I could drive all over the country and never have to come home."

He sighed again and rolled his shoulder a little restlessly, uncertain why he was revealing all this to Katie, when it was the kind of stuff he never even wanted to think about himself. "Eventually," he finally continued, "I decided I wanted to be a boxer."

When he said nothing to elaborate upon that decision, she asked quietly, "Why a boxer?"

He, too, rolled to his stomach, so that he could meet her gaze levelly. "Because, just once, I wanted to beat the hell out of my old man before he beat the hell out of me."

Something darkened in her eyes then, but for the life of him, Cooper couldn't say what.

"Your father hit you?" Her voice was so soft, he scarcely heard the question.

He nodded. "Yeah."

He waited for her to be outraged, waited for her to start expressing her righteous indignation and fawning over him as if he were still that frightened, hurt child. He waited for her to start mothering him, to start psychoanalyzing him, to start backing away from him as if he were serial killer material.

Instead, she only said softly, "I can't understand people who do that to their kids. Even before I became a mother, that sort of thing was reprehensible to me. Now that I have Andy, though, I find it even more difficult to understand. He's just a kid, you know? Who'd want to hurt a kid? Why would you hit someone so much smaller and more defenseless? How could a person live with themselves after doing something like that?"

Good questions, he thought. But he was able to offer no answers.

"I'm sorry your dad was like that," she added quietly. "You're too nice a guy to have had to go through that. I'm glad you didn't grow up to be just like him."

Cooper hesitated only a moment before saying, "Who says I didn't grow up to be just like him?"

Her expression when her eyes met his again was one of stark disbelief. "You're kidding, right?"

He shook his head. "Nope."

She chuckled once, but it was a nervous sound, not a happy one. "How can you say that? Cooper, you're the gentlest, kindest man I've ever met. The most decent human being I've ever encountered."

His laughter came quickly, raucously, and from the very depths of his soul. "Right," he managed to say when he regained his composure. "Gentle and kind. Yeah."

She shook her head in apparent disbelief. "It's true. How many other guys go out driving around in a blizzard to help other people for no other reason than that they just happen to be in a position to do it? How many other guys would take in a terrified woman and her child without a second thought, even when they didn't get a decent explanation for why they needed a place to stay? That's what good guys do, Cooper. And you're one of them."

He laughed some more, but finally regained enough control to reel himself in. "Well, Katie, if that's what you want to believe about me, you're certainly entitled to your opinion. Or your fantasy, as would be more accurate in this instance."

"Cooper—"

Before she could add anything to her ridiculous sentiment, Cooper jumped up and retreated to the kitchen. He cursed the small size of his apartment as he started opening and closing cabinet doors, searching for something as if he actually knew what he was looking for. He used to like the fact that his place was so tiny. Made it easier to clean up. Now, of course, he realized something else about having so little room.

Living in close quarters made people say and do the damnedest things.

Seven

Katie was going stir-crazy. She hadn't been outside the walls of Cooper's apartment for five days, and if she didn't get some fresh air and a change of scenery soon, she was definitely going to go mad. She missed being able to come and go as she pleased. She missed the simple act of walking barefoot through the grass. She missed eating lunch outdoors, under the awning of a small café. She missed hearing other people's voices raised in avid conversation, missed sitting in a dark movie theater enjoying the anticipation as the film credits rolled by, missed recreational shopping.

She missed being touched by someone other than a baby.

What made matters worse was that Cooper's apartment was just so boring. No color, no accents, no detail...no heart and no soul. There were no books for her to peruse, no souvenirs under glass that might tell her of his travels, no collections of things to make her ponder the source of his passion for such items. There were no photographs of his friends or family, no mementos of his life experiences, nothing to offer even a scrap of what he was like under his beautiful exterior.

How could he stand living in such a place? she wondered. She'd been dirt poor when she'd lived in Las Vegas, but she'd still had a nice place. Granted, the furnishings had been secondhand and third-rate, but she'd added warmth and color to them with her personal belongings and some treasured bits and pieces of her past. Cooper's place...

Cooper's place was like a hotel room. He could walk away from here with a single suitcase and never miss a thing. Then again, she thought, maybe that was the whole point. Maybe he didn't own anything or keep anything because he simply didn't want to become too attached to anything.

Or maybe he wasn't able to.

She didn't know why that thought struck her so soundly. Nor did she understand why it troubled her so. Even if she thought for a moment that Cooper would welcome her intrusion into his life—and, of course, she knew he would not—she had her own problems she needed to sort out before she could even begin to start working on someone else's.

Like how she was going to keep herself from going nuts in her self-imposed prison.

"Andy, buddy, I love you," she said to the baby who, as always, lay in the middle of Cooper's living room. "But I've got to get out of here for a while. What do you say? Want to go for a ride in the Snugli?"

Andy kicked his little legs vigorously, jerked his arms up and down wildly and cooed like there was no tomorrow.

Katie laughed. "Sounds like a big yes to me."

Glancing down at her baggy khaki shorts and oversize white T-shirt, she decided she looked suitably nondescript and nothing at all as she had the last time William had seen her more than nine weeks ago. And, hey, why would he be looking for her in Pennsauken anyway? Until she'd started searching for Cooper, Katie had never even heard of Pennsauken. South Jersey was a complete mystery to her, just as Philadelphia had been when William had first brought her there. All the more reason, she told herself now, to get out and explore her new surroundings.

She gathered her hair in a stubby ponytail and shrugged into the Snugli, arranging its crisscross, padded straps over her back before tucking Andy inside. Because the sun outside was high in the sky, she dropped a canvas, floppy-brimmed hat onto the baby's head and settled a pair of sunglasses on her nose. Then, checking to make sure she had change for the bus and enough money for lunch, she stuffed her wallet into her pocket, slung Andy's diaper bag over her shoulder, and headed for the front door.

She hesitated for a moment before turning the knob. Five days in one place without setting foot outside the door made a person feel a little attached to it. Or maybe it was just that, after having had Cooper around so close lately, Katie felt funny going anywhere alone. Of course, she wasn't alone, she reminded herself, glancing down at the infant affixed to her abdomen. But as cute as Andy was, he wouldn't be much help if she found herself in trouble.

Nonsense, she added to herself. She was perfectly safe. Good heavens, she was probably in more trouble being trapped in such close confines with Cooper than she would be anywhere else. The way that man made her feel . . . The things she found herself wanting to do with him . . . The dreams she'd been having at night . . .

She'd actually crept out of his bedroom one night and stood in the living room over the couch watching him sleep. She didn't know what had made her do something like that. She'd just awakened from a dream about him, a dream that became too fuzzy to remember clearly the moment she woke up, and for some reason, she hadn't been able to resist the urge to make sure he was okay.

He'd been lying on his back, naked to the waist, the sheet with which he'd covered himself dipping well below the waistband of his white cotton briefs. He had thrown an arm up over his head so that it lay in an arc on the armrest of the sofa. His chest had risen and fallen with the slow, steady respiration of deep slumber, and she had been fascinated by the thick scattering of blond hair that covered it. Her fingers had itched to bury themselves in the light curls, to trace the pattern across his chest and down his torso to where it thinned in a straight line that disappeared into his briefs.

She must have made some soft sound, because he'd suddenly stirred in his sleep and rolled to his side. A single, straight shaft of blond hair had fallen forward over his eyes, and before she'd realized what she was doing, Katie had dropped her hand to brush the lock back in place. Cooper had sighed in his sleep and mumbled something she wasn't able to understand. And all she'd been able to think was that she wished she could curl up right beside him.

"You definitely need to get out for a while," she said to herself aloud. "Because you clearly are losing your mind."

Without a second thought, she gripped the doorknob and turned it, then stepped across the threshold and pulled the door shut behind her. Only then did it occur to her that she didn't have a key to get back inside. She knew Cooper would be home from work by four-thirty, and it was nearly two o'clock now. The diaper bag contained diapers, wipes, a change of clothes and two bottles of water, and Andy had just had a late lunch. She and her son would be fine.

Unconcerned by her predicament, Katie headed for the bus stop where she'd stepped from a bus five days ago, ready for an adventure and happy to be alive.

It was the quiet that struck Cooper when he opened his front door later that afternoon. Usually, when he came home from work, Katie had the stereo on and tuned to the jazz station, and more often than not, she was singing along to whatever old standard was playing. Yesterday, he'd interrupted her dancing around the living room with Andy in her arms, mother and baby both laughing in time to a rowdy rendition of some bluesy saxophone number. They'd turned around when they heard him come in, and Katie had cried out over the music, "Hi! Welcome home!"

Her greeting had made Cooper feel funny inside. Made him feel as if he'd come to the wrong place. Made him feel as if he wanted to go out and come in again and receive exactly the same greeting.

But today, his apartment was as silent as it used to be. Back before Katie and Andy had brought it to life.

"Katie?" he called out.

When he received no response to his summons, an odd heat licked at his belly. "Katie?" he tried again. But again, only silence met his question.

He pushed the door closed softly behind him, then went to his bedroom. Her duffel bag was still squatting in the corner, and Andy's quilt was folded neatly at the foot of Cooper's bed. Only when he realized she hadn't packed up and left him did he realize his heart rate had gone through the roof. He closed his eyes and inhaled deeply a few times to steady it.

And he told himself not to panic.

There was obviously no sign of forced entry into the apartment, and no indication that Katie had left under anything other than her own steam and of her own free will. But where on earth could she have gone?

Still wondering about that, Cooper began to undress. But before he was even halfway done unbuttoning his shirt, he went to the living room and turned on the stereo. The woman's voice that crooned out from the speakers was nowhere near as smoky and sexy as Katie's was, but for now, he decided, it would do. At least it covered the silence that made him feel so edgy.

He was still shirtless and tugging on his blue jeans when his doorbell chimed loudly. Without bothering to fasten the top button, he raced to the front door and threw it open.

Katie stood on the other side, wearing Andy around her middle in one of those contraptions Cooper had seen women wearing from time to time to transport their offspring. Behind her stood a big, burly man in a sweat-stained work shirt, peeking out at him through the rungs of a rocking chair he carried upside down atop his head.

"Hi, Cooper!" Katie said enthusiastically when she saw him. "I'm sorry, but I forgot I didn't have a key to your place until I was already locked out."

She pushed past him, paving the way for her massive companion, and called cheerily over her shoulder to the huge man, "You can just put it in the living room, Conrad."

"Conrad?" Cooper asked before he could stop himself.

The man stooped to move himself and his burden through the door, then set the rocking chair down where Katie had instructed with all the gentleness and finesse of cellist. Then he turned around and extended his hand to Cooper. "Conrad DiStefano, fine antiques," he said with a smile.

"Conrad?" Cooper repeated.

"Sure, you can call me Conrad. Just don't call me late for dinner. Knowuddamean?"

Cooper opened his mouth to say something else, but Katie cut him off.

"Isn't it wonderful?" she said, motioning toward the rocking chair. "I found it at Pennsauken Mart. Did you know about this place, Cooper? It's incredible. Andy and I spent two hours there, and we still didn't see the whole thing. Conrad's one of the vendors. He has a great little antique shop. I absolutely fell in love with this rocking chair—it's almost exactly like one my grandmother had when I was a girl. He let me have it for a song."

"How much is a song?" Cooper asked.

She looked puzzled for a moment, then smiled. "No, I mean he let me have it for a *song*. Literally."

"'Stardust,'" Conrad told him. "It's always been one of my favorites. My Ginny and me danced to it at our wedding forty-six years ago next month. Katie did it beautiful."

"Isn't that sweet?" she said.

"Of course," Conrad added, "when she told me she didn't have a rocking chair for that little guy of hers, well...I thought it was a crime. Ginny and me just about wore our rocking chair out getting our six little ones to sleep when they were babies."

"Six?" Cooper asked incredulously.

Conrad nodded and punched the air with an eager fist. "You bet. Every last one is an engineer now. Every last one. Of course, it would be nice if they didn't take their work so serious all the time. It'd be nice to have a coupla grandkids running around. But I guess I have to respect their lifestyles, you know? At least Mikey and his Laura are talkin' about it now. So maybe by Christmas, we'll hear some news, who knows?"

The surrealism of the moment began to wash over Cooper, and all he could do was mutter, "Um...you, uh...you must be very proud."

The other man nodded vigorously. "You know it. Lisa's an aeronautical engineer, Benny's a mechanical engineer, Paulie's a civil engineer—he's one of those guys who build bridges, you know—and Mindy, the little one, she's—"

"Um, no offense, Mr. DiStefano, but—"

"Call me Conrad, please."

"No offense, Conrad, but Katie and I should—"

"Say no more." Conrad held up a hand. "I gotta get back to the store anyway. Thanks, Katie," he added, lifting a hand in farewell.

"Oh, no, Conrad, thank *you*," she gushed back. "You and Ginny both. Make sure she takes care of that ankle, okay?"

"You betcha."

"And remember what I told you about linseed oil, okay? It really works wonders on bird's-eye maple."

"No problem. You bring that little guy back for a visit real soon, you hear?"

"Next week, I promise."

With a final duck of his head in farewell, the other man exited, pulling the front door closed behind him. Cooper stared at it for a moment before turning around to address Katie. She eyed him expectantly, her face a silent question mark. He opened his mouth to speak, closed it again, then turned to look at the front door once more, not completely sure he hadn't just imagined the entire exchange that had just occurred. Then he looked at Katie again.

"What?" she asked him.

"What the hell was that all about?"

"What do you mean?"

"Just how the hell did you spend your afternoon?"

"I went shopping."

"You went shopping."

She nodded. "Uh-huh. Why? What's wrong?"

What's wrong? Cooper repeated her question to himself. What's wrong? What was wrong was that he'd come home from work to find her gone and had been terrified he'd never see her again. What was wrong was that just when he was starting to think something terrible had happened to her and Andy, she'd come strolling in with her new best buddy as if nothing in the world were amiss.

What was wrong was that she'd brought a piece of furniture into his apartment that had no business being there. And what was really wrong was that Cooper didn't mind it for a moment that there was a rocking chair—a *rocking chair*—sitting in the middle of his living room for all the world to see.

"Um..." he began. He wove his fingers through his hair, smoothing his palm over the crown of his head in a restless gesture. "Do you do this kind of thing often?"

She continued to look at him, clearly puzzled. "What kind of thing?"

He eyed her for a moment longer before elaborating, "Make friends with total strangers?"

Katie shrugged, not sure she liked his tone of voice. He was obviously angry with her for some reason, and she couldn't understand why. She hadn't done anything wrong. She'd gone shopping, she'd seen the rocking chair, and she'd struck up a conversation with Conrad and his wife. The next thing she'd known, she was bartering for the piece of furniture, Conrad was offering to drive her and her new acquisition home, and she was giving him Cooper's address.

She hadn't stopped to think about the fact that this wasn't her home. That she had no home. Until now.

"Well, no, not exactly," she said in response to his question. "I mean . . . Conrad and Ginny didn't feel like strangers when I started talking to them. They were really nice, and . . ."

She wanted to tell Cooper that the DiStefanos had reminded Katie of her own parents. That the sight of the rocking chair had carried her back to her own youth, to the small house in western Kentucky where she'd grown up, to a time when her life had been so simple, so carefree, so happy. It had been such a long time since anyone had been so kind to her. Something deep inside her that had been buried since she'd left home so many years ago had swelled to life, and she'd remembered what it was like to be cared about, to feel human.

She hadn't realized how easy it was to forget the things that were truly important. Like simply making a friend.

But instead of telling Cooper all those things, she only continued softly, "The rocking chair cost me nothing. And I can use it. It's tough to rock Andy to sleep on your bed. It won't take up much room, and it doesn't make any noise. You probably won't even notice it's here."

NO COST! NO OBLIGATION TO BUY!
NO PURCHASE NECESSARY!

PLAY "LUCKY 7"
AND GET FIVE FREE GIFTS!

HOW TO PLAY:

1. With a coin, carefully scratch off the silver box at the right. Then check the claim chart to see what we have for you—FREE BOOKS and a gift—ALL YOURS! ALL FREE!

2. Send back this card and you'll receive brand-new Silhouette Desire® novels. These books have a cover price of $3.50 each, but they are yours to keep absolutely free.

3. There's no catch. You're under no obligation to buy anything. We charge nothing—ZERO—for your first shipment. And you don't have to make any minimum number of purchases—not even one!

4. The fact is thousands of readers enjoy receiving books by mail from the Silhouette Reader Service™ months before they're available in stores. They like the convenience of home delivery and they love our discount prices!

5. We hope that after receiving your free books you'll want to remain a subscriber. But the choice is yours—to continue or cancel, anytime at all! So why not take us up on our invitation, with no risk of any kind. You'll be glad you did!

This beautiful porcelain box is topped with a lovely bouquet of porcelain flowers, perfect for holding rings, pins or other precious trinkets — and is yours absolutely free when you accept our no risk offer!

NOT ACTUAL SIZE

PLAY "LUCKY 7"

**Just scratch off the silver box with a coin.
Then check below to see the gifts you get.**

YES! I have scratched off the silver box. Please send me all the gifts for which I qualify. I understand I am under no obligation to purchase any books, as explained on the back and on the opposite page.

225 CIS A3JA
(U-SIL-D-08/96)

NAME

ADDRESS   APT.

CITY   STATE   ZIP

Offer limited to one per household and not valid to current Silhouette Desire® subscribers. All orders subject to approval.

DETACH AND MAIL CARD TODAY

THE SILHOUETTE READER SERVICE™: HERE'S HOW IT WORKS

Accepting free books places you under no obligation to buy anything. You may keep the books and gift and return the shipping statement marked "cancel". If you do not cancel, about a month later we'll send you 6 additional novels, and bill you just $2.90 each plus 25¢ delivery and applicable sales tax, if any.* That's the complete price–and compared to cover prices of $3.50 each–quite a bargain! You may cancel at any time, but if you choose to continue, every month we'll send you 6 more books, which you may either purchase at the discount price…or return to us and cancel your subscription.

*Terms and prices subject to change without notice. Sales tax applicable in N.Y.

If offer card is missing, write to: Silhouette Reader Service, 3010 Walden Ave, PO Box 1867, Buffalo, NY 14240-1867

BUSINESS REPLY MAIL
FIRST-CLASS MAIL   PERMIT NO. 717   BUFFALO, NY

POSTAGE WILL BE PAID BY ADDRESSEE

SILHOUETTE READER SERVICE
3010 WALDEN AVE
PO BOX 1867
BUFFALO NY 14240-9952

NO POSTAGE
NECESSARY
IF MAILED
IN THE
UNITED STATES

He studied her in silence for a moment longer, his hands settled firmly on his trim hips, the sight of his bare chest rising and falling with each breath he took wreaking all sorts of havoc on her senses. He cupped a hand over his mouth, then rubbed it uneasily over his jaw.

Finally, he asked, "And just what are you planning to do with it when it's time for you to leave?"

Only then did Katie realize what she had done. She hadn't for a moment considered that. She hadn't consciously remembered that she would be leaving Cooper's place, and very soon at that. Only when he threw the reminder up in her face did she understand why he was angry. He thought her act of bringing the rocking chair into his home was an implied request to stay here indefinitely. And he'd made it clear to her on more than one occasion that her presence here was only temporary.

"You can keep it after I leave," she said softly. "I won't be out anything. You could use a couple more pieces of furniture anyway. No offense, Cooper, but your apartment isn't the warmest place in the world."

"I don't want it," he told her frankly, ignoring the rest of her comment.

"Then you can sell it. Or just hang on to it until I get settled somewhere, and I'll send for it."

She could tell by the expression on his face that he didn't like that idea, either. But he said nothing. Andy began to fret in the Snugli, and Katie knew he was getting hungry. Nevertheless, she only stood there staring at Cooper, wishing things could be different between them. Finally, the baby's fretting turned into a steady cry of demand, and she hoisted him up out of his sling before unhooking it at her sides.

"I have to change Andy's diaper and feed him," she told Cooper quietly without looking at him. "Excuse me."

She walked hastily into the bedroom, closing the door behind her, and deposited both baby and diaper bag in the middle of the bed. She had just fastened Andy into a fresh diaper and had freed one arm from her sleeve in preparation for feeding him, when a soft rap came on the bedroom door.

Katie paused before removing her other arm from the other sleeve and called out, "Yes?"

The door opened inward slowly, and Cooper appeared, carrying the rocking chair. Without saying a word, he went to the corner of the bedroom, the one by the window, and situated the chair so that whoever was sitting there could look through the open blinds at the softly rippling leaves of the dogwood tree outside. He straightened and turned to meet Katie's gaze levelly for a moment, then, again without speaking, crossed the room and exited, pulling the door closed behind him.

Katie watched him go with a mixture of so many emotions bubbling through her. And as she pulled her T-shirt up over her head and opened the flap of her nursing bra, she wondered how on earth she was ever going to be able to leave Cooper behind when it came time for her and Andy to go.

Thunder rumbled loudly outside the window, and Cooper turned restlessly to his side to watch the rain spatter the glass. The glow of the street lamp on the other side refracted in the tiny droplets of water, making them shine like diamonds against the night-colored glass. He had awakened thirty minutes ago to the sound of Andy's hungry cries, and he hadn't been able to go back to sleep. The storm had begun between then and now, first as a simple late spring shower, then quickly growing into one of those rowdy deluges that seemed to go on forever.

A quick series of lightning flashes illuminated the living room a few times, then threw it into darkness again. More thunder rolled across the sky, starting in the distance and gradually drawing nearer, before exploding in a booming cacophony seemingly right above Cooper's roof.

He had always liked storms for some reason. The more violent, the better. Something about nature's fury reassured him in some way. It was nice to know there were one or two things that were beyond the control of man. One or two things that would never submit, no matter how long or how hard people tried to make them.

He heard a soft sound punch through the darkness, and he trained his gaze away from the window at the exact moment another burst of lightning lit the room. It flashed just long enough to allow him to see Katie standing framed by his bedroom doorway. In that split second of illumination, he noted that she was wearing a big, loose, man-styled shirt to sleep in, its sleeves rolled to her elbows, its length scarcely covering her to midthigh. Then the darkness thankfully descended again, and he could tell himself he'd only imagined the terror in her eyes.

"I hate storms," she whispered, crossing her arms over her breasts, and rubbing her shoulders nervously. "They scare me to death."

Cooper sat up on the sofa and tugged the sheet more securely around his waist. "Why?"

She crossed the room toward him, quickening her pace when another bout of thunder shook the building. "I don't know. I just always have. All that unleashed power. All that raging wind that defies control."

He smiled. "I was just lying here thinking that that's what I *like* about storms."

"Well, not me."

She stood there staring at him, clearly wanting him to ask her to join him, which, Cooper knew, was the last thing he should do. He was nearly naked, she was nearly naked, Andy was sleeping full and sated in the other room, it was dark, it was stormy, it was romantic....

"So, you want to stay out here for a little while?" he heard himself asking.

She nodded vigorously. "Uh-huh."

He sat up and reached behind himself for his pillow, punched it up, then returned it to its original place and scooted back to lean against it. He drew his knees up in front of him to create an empty spot at the other end of the couch. Immediately, Katie moved to take it, pulling her feet up onto the cushion to curl herself into a ball.

"Thanks," she said.

"No problem."

Instead of abating, the storm began to rage more fiercely, and he could see her discomfort grow with every passing moment. She began to rock her body back and forth and hum an erratic tune.

"You really *like* storms?" she finally asked incredulously.

"Yep. You're really afraid of them?"

"Yeah."

"Then I guess it's a good thing you're in here, and not out there."

"I guess so."

Although, at the moment, Katie thought as she sneaked another peek at Cooper from the corner of her eye, that point might be debatable. She knew he slept in nothing but his briefs, and wondered if even that much cover was something he'd simply begun to adopt recently in light of her own presence in his apartment.

As had been the case during her illicit, secret perusal of him as he slept a few nights ago, she was once again fascinated by the splash of blond hair on his chest—not to mention his chest itself, solid and corded with muscle as it was. The top of the sheet rested just above his navel, but she knew his belly was flat and taut, just begging for the gentle touch of a hand to prove it. He had bent his arms to rest the back of his head in his hands, and in the scant ray of light from the street lamp outside the window, she could easily trace the line of his big biceps swelled in poetic arcs.

Katie had to stifle the sigh that wanted to erupt from somewhere deep inside her. Instead, she reluctantly dragged her gaze away from Cooper and stared into the vague darkness of the living room instead.

"I saw that," she heard him say quietly from beside her.

A flare of heat ignited in her midsection and spread quickly to parts of her that in no way needed warming. "Saw what?" she asked him.

"That not-so-subtle inventory you just took."

"I don't know what you're talking about."

"Knock it off, Katie. It won't wash."

She turned to gaze at him fully. "What won't wash?"

He shook his head slowly, as if he really didn't want to say what he was about to say. "Ever since you showed up here...hell, even before that...ever since the night I walked into your place in Chestnut Hill, there's been something burning up the air between us. If you deny it, I'll call you a liar, and you'll know I'm right."

She settled her chin atop one knee and continued to stare at him. "Okay. I admit it. I think you're very attractive."

"I think I turn you on."

That funny heat inside her began to rage hotter. "Okay," she conceded hesitantly. "You turn me on."

"You turn me on, too."

She licked her lips nervously, uncertain what she should say. As far as Cooper knew, she was a married woman. He'd said himself it was the only thing keeping him at a distance, and that such a distance was tenuous at best. What would happen if she gave him that explanation she owed him and revealed the fact that she wasn't married? she wondered. What would happen if he found out she wasn't tied—neither morally, nor emotionally, nor legally—to another man? What would happen if he knew she was his for the taking?

Don't be an idiot, she told herself. *You know very well what would happen. And you'd love every minute of it.*

"Cooper," she began, still not sure what she was going to tell him.

But he cut her off before either of them could find out. "And I hope you appreciate the colossal effort I'm making to be sure that husband of yours doesn't have any ammunition of the adultery variety to stick you with, should the two of you end up not being able to resolve your—what did you call it?—oh, yeah...your *marital difficulties*...and wind up in divorce court. But then, that's just the kind of guy I am."

"Cooper—"

"Kind, I mean. Gentle. Decent. That sort of thing."

"Cooper—"

"That is what you called me, isn't it, Katie? Decent?"

"Cooper—" she tried again.

"Lucky thing, too, I'd say. Otherwise, right about now, we'd probably be engaged in something we have no business being engaged in. Wouldn't you say so?"

She knew she should tell him to cut it out. Better yet, she knew she should just stand up and march right back to his bedroom, back to where Andrew still slept so soundly, so conveniently. She knew she shouldn't tell him what she really wanted to tell him.

Nevertheless, the words that came out when she opened her mouth were, "He's not my husband."

Eight

    "**W**hat did you say?" Cooper held his breath as he awaited Katie's response. He was afraid to believe he'd heard her correctly, was still half-certain he had misunderstood.

    "I said…" She inhaled a breath that was none too steady and released it slowly. "I said he's not my husband."

    Instead of saying anything, he dropped his gaze to the ring encircling the fourth finger of her left hand. Her gaze followed his, and when she saw where it was directed, she spread her fingers open wide and eyed the piece of jewelry blandly.

    "Yes, it's a wedding band, and he gave it to me at a wedding ceremony. But the only reason I'm still wearing it is because I might need the money I could get from it in hock." Her gaze settled steadfastly on Cooper's again. "William's not my husband," she repeated. "He never was. When he married me, he already had a wife. He just neglected to tell me—or the minister, or the state of Nevada, or anyone else—about her at the time."

She sighed heavily, then reached for the ring with her right hand. With trembling fingers, she twisted the piece of jewelry until she had removed it completely. Then she eyed it carelessly and set it on the end table beside the couch.

"He's not my husband," she said again. "He never was."

Cooper didn't realize he had clenched his hands into fists until his fingers gradually began to uncurl, and he felt the pinpricks of sensation replacing the numbness that had set in. He had scarcely heard the details of her husband's bigamy, because one thought kept pounding at his brain, over and over again.

Katie's not married. Not married, not married . . .

This time he was the one to sigh unevenly. "How . . . how did you find out the truth?" he managed to ask.

She chuckled anxiously. "His, um, his wife came to see me the night before Andy was born. His real wife. She and William had gotten into an argument that afternoon, just before he'd left on a business trip that was, for once, actually a business trip. At some point during their fight, he told her about me. Told her about his plan. That's why I was packing to leave. I had to get away before William got back from his trip."

"His plan? What plan?"

Katie stood and began to pace, but the small confines of the living room prevented her from going far. She crossed to one wall in five easy strides, spun quickly around, and then repeated the motion. Then she did it again. She paced as she spoke, her steps seeming modulated by the words she said.

"William's wife isn't able to have kids. Something about a childhood illness that left her sterile. They didn't find out about it until they saw a fertility specialist to see why she hadn't gotten pregnant after a year of trying."

She finally stopped pacing and dropped onto the sofa beside Cooper again, burying her fingers in her hair, her face in her hands. "William really wants to have kids," she continued. "He *really* wants them. Especially a son. The realization that his wife couldn't give him any evidently made him a little crazy."

Still clenching her hair in her fists, she turned her head to look Cooper right in the eye. "When she came to see me, she had a black eye and a fat lip. She told me she fell. I knew she was lying. But I don't know if William beat her up because she fought with him about me, or if it was something that happened on a regular basis. Maybe it was because she couldn't give him the children he wanted—I don't know. All I know is that, at some point, William became obsessed with the idea of having a child. So obsessed, that he broke the law and completely ignored anyone's feelings but his own."

"He went looking for a brood mare," Cooper threw in, surprised he was able to keep his voice level.

Katie nodded, but didn't change her position. "Actually, to be fair, I don't know if he had a plan already mapped out when he met me, or if meeting me—someone with no roots, no family and nowhere to turn if things got ugly—gave him the idea. But yeah, more or less, he went looking for a brood mare," she repeated dismally. "One who was so naive, and so stupid and so gullible, she'd believe a man like him could actually fall in love with her and make her his wife." She turned her head to bury her face once again in her hands. "And I just happened to be that naive, stupid and gullible."

"Katie—"

She cut him off before he could say more. "As I look back on it now, I can hardly believe I fell for it. I was working as a waitress, and William came into the diner one night and sat at one of my tables. He was obviously wealthy and very successful, and so, so handsome. He had no cause to want anything to do with someone like me. Like I said, for all I know, he came up with his plan right there on the spot, while he was talking to me. He flirted with me, and I was dazzled by him. Next thing I knew, I was having dinner with him. A week later, we were married.''

She moved her feet to the floor and dangled her hands between her knees, staring at the carpet. "At least, I *thought* we were married. I thought I was living out one of those rags-to-riches, whirlwind romances you read about in the supermarket tabloids." She lifted her hands to frame the headline she was imagining. "'Millionaire Gives Waitress A Tip to Last A Lifetime!'"

Then she dropped her hands to her lap again and tangled her fingers together. "I thought I was being rewarded somehow for some good deed I'd done in my life. I thought..." She emitted another humorless chuckle. "I guess I was just too trusting of him. You're right, Cooper. I do make fast friends with strangers. I should know better. I never stopped to think there was something sinister to William. Boy, was I a sap."

As if unable to sit still and talk at the same time, she rose once more and began to cover the room in a restless circle. "It all makes sense now. I don't know why I didn't realize there was something wrong before it all went bust."

"What all makes sense now?"

"When we moved to Philadelphia, William and I almost never went out. I figured it was because we were newlyweds, and he just wanted to stay home with me and feel like we were a family. Especially since I got pregnant shortly after we got...shortly after the wedding. I thought he craved privacy because he was wealthy and prominent in the community. I just thought..."

She sighed deeply. "Actually, I guess I didn't think at all. What few friends of William's I met seemed a little shady, at best. I never felt comfortable around them. And he was gone more often than he was home, traveling on business, he told me, but now, of course, I know he was with his real wife. At his real home. He was just biding his time until I had our baby, then he was going to take Andy away from me and never let me see my son again.''

Cooper said nothing for a moment, simply sat still and let his brain process all the information Katie had given him. In a way, it was a perfectly credible story. But it was also the stuff of a bad television miniseries.

''So you're telling me this guy—William—met you in Vegas, faked a marriage to you, got you pregnant, and brought you back to Philadelphia so he could take the baby away from you when you had it, and then pretend you didn't exist?'' He rubbed his forehead hard. ''You'll excuse me if I have a little trouble swallowing this story. I mean, Katie... face it. There are a million holes in it.''

She stopped her pacing, but stared out the rain-spattered window. ''Don't you think I know how unbelievable it all sounds? Don't you think I spent a lot of time trying to convince myself the woman who came to my door was just some crazy bimbo who was in love with William, and trying to wreck his marriage in some weird, *Fatal Attraction* replay? I know I sound like a lunatic, Cooper, but...'' Her expression was desperate when she turned to face him again. ''But that's exactly the way it is. That's why I need a place to hide. Because the minute William Winslow finds me, he'll take Andy away from me, and I'll never see my son again.''

Cooper shook his head. ''Katie, he can't take Andy away from you. Are you kidding? After what he's done, no judge in the country is going to let him come near your son. He's a bigamist, a wife beater, a liar.... Hell, you've probably got enough you could charge him with to make him do jail time.''

Katie slumped forward, as if in defeat. ''You really don't get it, do you, Cooper?''

''Get what?''

''William's rich. He's powerful. He's got so many people in his pocket, there's no room for lint.''

''So?''

She sighed and returned to the sofa. "So he's also a big liar who's got more credibility than my honest version of the facts ever would."

"What do you mean?"

"Here's what I gathered from my little chat with his wife. William paid off the reverend in Vegas so that any record of our wedding and any witnesses who might have been there have disappeared. And he was careful that our names were never connected in Philadelphia. My bank account was in my name alone. Any purchases he made for me were made in cash. The town house is in his name, but it's a residence he'll claim he bought for those occasions when he works late and doesn't want to make the long drive to his home in Bucks County. There's absolutely no evidence out there that connects the two of us in any way."

"Except for Andy," she said on a quiet sigh. "And once William finds me, he intends to sue me for custody."

"And who says he'll get it?"

"Oh, he'll get it. He's got all kinds of buddies in the legal system. He'll have me painted as an unfit mother with no problem. I'm a nobody from nowhere who was working as a waitress in a diner when I met him. He'll say he was in Vegas on business when he met me, that *I* came on to him, and in a moment of weakness, he succumbed to me. He'll put on his sad, chastened face and admit that he made a mistake, but that he's ready to take responsibility for it by doing right by the child he fathered, raising Andy with all the benefits due a legitimate son.

"I, on the other hand, will come across as a desperate, uneducated woman with loose morals, one who slept with a man she barely knew and who has absolutely no way to take care of a child. It's William's word against mine. And he has a lot more influence and a lot more friends and a lot more credibility than I do."

Almost ruthlessly, she ticked off the rest of her shortcomings on one hand with the index finger of the other. "I have no relatives, no money, no job, no home, and no way to support my son. William is wealthy, prominent, successful and can offer his son a seemingly stable, happy home. You tell me who the judge is going to favor in a situation like that. Especially a judge who's on William's payroll.''

Cooper had to acknowledge that she had a point. ''What about his wife?'' he finally asked. ''She could back you up.''

Katie shook her head. ''William's wife is too terrified of him to contradict anything he says or have him charged with battery. She won't come to my rescue.''

''She came to your rescue when she told you about William's plan.''

''That's just because she didn't want to be forced to raise another woman's child—a child her husband fathered during an adulterous affair. A child that just rubs her nose in the fact that she'll never have any of her own. The only reason she came to see me was because she wanted me out of the picture, and she suspected I'd leave once she told me what William had planned.''

''If William wins custody of Andy, his wife is going to wind up being the one to raise him,'' Cooper observed. ''If she hates the idea enough to risk William's wrath in coming to warn you, then maybe she'll risk it again by speaking up in a court of law.''

''Maybe,'' Katie conceded after a moment's thought. ''But I'm not willing to take the chance.''

''So you're stuck.''

''I'm stuck.''

Unless...

Cooper halted the thought as quickly as it entered his brain. *No way, man,* he immediately instructed himself. *Not in a million years.*

There was no way he was going to tell Katie she could keep his name on Andy's birth certificate, thereby voiding William's claim to fatherhood and assuming paternity himself. Although he understood now why she had named him as Andy's father instead of her supposed husband, there was no way Cooper was going to agree to be responsible for a son who wasn't his.

Even disregarding all the legal and moral hoo-ha that would go along with such an act, the fathering gene in Cooper's DNA was more than a little faulty. There wasn't a Dugan man in his family tree who had been anything other than lousy at parenting. At best, they ignored their children. At worst, they hurt them. And Cooper, for one, was going to make sure the cycle ended with him.

"Unless what?" Katie asked.

Only then did he realize he'd spoken his initial, one-word objection aloud. "There must be some way to work this out," he said hastily, hoping to cover his gaffe.

"Believe me, Cooper, if there was some way to work this out, I would have found it by now. And the only resolution I can find is hiding from William until Andy is eighteen."

"And just how do you propose to do that?"

"Don't worry," she told him as she pushed herself up off the sofa and began to pace again. "I'm not planning on staying here for that length of time. I know we're in your way, and I know you can't wait to be rid of us. I'll figure out something. Just give me another week. That will give me long enough to rest and make some arrangements. Andy and I will be out of your hair after that, I'll do whatever is necessary to correct the information on his birth certificate. Then I promise we'll never bother you again."

"Katie, that's not what I meant."

"Wasn't it?"

Cooper stood, too, quickly remembered that he was wearing nothing but a pair of briefs, and jerked the sheet free of the sofa cushions to wind it around his middle. He crossed the room slowly, pausing just behind her. Without even thinking about what he was doing, he cupped his hands over her shoulders and gently squeezed.

"No. I just meant..." He just meant what? he asked himself. He had no idea what to think about all this. "You and Andy can stay here for as long as you need to. I told you that before. I just wish I could offer you some kind of assurance that everything will work out."

"Don't worry about it," she mumbled without turning around. "It's not your problem." She cleared her throat and sniffled, then scrubbed a finger under her nose.

Gently, Cooper urged her body around so she could look at him, only to wish that he hadn't. Even in the scarce light available, he could see that her gray eyes were brighter and seemed almost transparent, thanks to the presence of unspilled tears. She had knifed her fingers through her dark hair so many times during their conversation, that it was swept back from her forehead in a tousled heap, framing her face in a mass of rampant curls.

"That's where you're wrong," he told her softly as he let his fingers follow the paths her own had made in her hair. "It *is* my problem. You and Andy both are. Ever since the night he was born, I've felt like..." He sighed, not sure he should reveal what he was about to tell her, but wanting her to know nonetheless.

"Like what?"

"Like I was responsible for you both. Like maybe the fates threw us together for a reason."

He cupped her jaw in one hand and tilted her head back to meet her gaze levelly. "When you disappeared from the hospital that morning, I felt like someone had stripped me of everything I owned. I don't know any other way to explain it. When I realized you and Andy were gone, it was like I'd lost something vitally important, and I hadn't even known you for a day."

As if he'd startled her by his confession, Katie parted her lips a fraction of an inch, and seemingly without realizing what she was doing, she touched the tip of her tongue to the corner of her mouth.

The simple gesture was Cooper's undoing. The litany that had pounded in his head earlier came back to remind him that she was a single woman. She wasn't tied to another man. The one obstacle that had been preventing him from acting on the almost irresistible urge to take her in the most basic, fiercest way imaginable was gone. An entire week's worth of desperate longing without being able to assuage it evaporated. Just like that. There was nothing to keep him from making love to Katie. Nothing but a refusal from Katie herself. And if the look in her eyes was any indication, that refusal was never going to come.

Before he even realized he was doing it, he lowered his head to hers and covered her mouth with his. Immediately, she responded, more zealously and recklessly than he ever would have imagined she could. Katie's kiss was filled with a desperation and loneliness that put his own to shame. What else could he do but kiss her back?

She tasted of sweetness and promise, of gentleness and faith. The moment he began to lose himself in that kiss, he knew he was going to regret it later.

Then even that thought dissolved, only to be replaced by a timeless desire and infinite need. Katie was soft in all the places Cooper was hard, generous in all the places he was lacking. He knew instinctively that she could fill the emptiness in his soul and warm the cold patches in his heart. She could be his salvation. She could be his hope. In one final coherent thought, he reminded himself not to let her get to him.

Then he kissed her again.

She clung to him, cupping one hand possessively over his nape to pull his head down more intently to her own, twining her fingers fiercely in the hair on his chest with the other. In turn, he roped an arm around her waist to hold her firm, and bunched a fistful of her hair in his hand. For long moments, they only urged each other closer, pressing their bodies together until they nearly fused into one being.

Then Cooper skimmed his hands lightly over Katie's face, down her neck and throat, and settled them between her breasts. When she deepened their kiss, he splayed his fingers over the soft mounds, taking one in each hand with a gentle pressure. He remembered that morning in the kitchen, when he had seen clearly their outline and generous peaks through the thin fabric of her nightshirt. He remembered how badly he had wanted to reach out and taste her.

He reached for the buttons of her shirt, and with fumbling fingers, unfastened them one by one. Within seconds, he shoved the garment aside and lifted his head from hers, to see that part of her that had kept him preoccupied for a week.

Not much to his surprise, Katie was even more beautiful than he had imagined she would be. Her breasts were heavy, dusky and round, the peaks agitated and stiff. Taking one in his hand, he lifted it to his mouth and drew inside as much as he could. His tongue flattened against her nipple for a brief second before he remembered that she was a nursing mother. Immediately, he pulled his head away, only to find that Katie had woven her fingers in his hair to keep him from retreating.

She pressed his head back against her, and assured him in a weak whisper, "It's okay. I like the way you feel there."

Cooper returned to his ministrations, but instead of suckling her, as his instincts bid him do, he traced his tongue along the underside of her breast, rubbed his mouth lightly over the peak, and dropped soft, butterfly kisses across the top. Then he moved to the other side and repeated each action. Katie's fingers tightened in his hair with every stroke of his tongue, then loosened to do it again.

He wasn't sure how long the two of them remained entwined in such a way—perhaps moments, perhaps hours. Sensation eclipsed time, and the only reality Cooper acknowledged was in what he could hold in his hands. He buried his face in Katie's neck and dragged his fingers down her back, curving his palms over the contours of her fanny and thighs, pressing intimately into her firm flesh. When she groaned out his name, he moved one hand up harder, cradling the damp warmth between her legs.

Her entire body jerked in response to the intimate invasion, but instead of moving away from his probing fingers, Katie brought her hips forward to facilitate a more thorough exploration. Cooper scraped his fingertips up over the damp, heated cotton of her panties, then immediately dipped his hand inside the fabric to bury his fingers in the soft thatch of curls he encountered. He carried his exploration lower still, until he found the hot core of her. Slowly, methodically, he tilled the warm furrows, moving his fingers in lazy circles and uneven lines.

Katie stilled as he touched her. Her breathing became shallow, her eyes closed, and her hands clung loosely to the sheet dipping low at his waist. Her head was tipped back just enough to allow Cooper to bend over her and brush his lips softly against hers. Then, without warning, a violent shudder shook her, and she cried out as she trembled around his hand.

"Oh," she murmured as another wave washed over her. "Oh, Cooper."

Unable to tolerate not being inside her, he dropped to his knees on the floor and pulled her down with him. Hastily, they shoved away what little clothing and covering remained, and reunited naked. She straddled his waist and reached behind herself, curling her fingers around his rigid shaft, cupping him as fully as she could in her palm. He lifted his hands to her breasts, fingering the tips as if they were gems. Then she rose and guided him toward her, settling herself slowly over him.

Cooper stilled to watch their union, feeling the warmth and comfort of Katie surrounding him as he disappeared inside her inch by inch. Slowly, she encompassed his full length, until he felt himself become a part of her entirely. He bucked and jerked beneath her, but the motion only made her possession of him more complete. Then slowly, she began to rise again, as if to free him, and unable to stop himself, he gripped her hips hard and brought her slamming down atop him again.

He rolled both their bodies until she lay beneath him, and only then did he feel as if he were restoring some halfhearted sense of control over the situation. But he still couldn't separate himself from her. Because he didn't *want* to separate himself from her. As far as Cooper was concerned, he could lie on his living room floor for the rest of his life while Katie Brennan offered him sanctuary in her warm body. If he never saw another sunrise, he would be content. Because all that mattered in that single moment was Katie and the way she made him feel.

Banishing the realization, he emptied his mind and pushed himself up on his knees. She curled her legs around his waist, and tangled her fingers with his. Cooper bent forward to trap her hands against the floor above her head, then thrust his entire body forward. This time he would be the possessor, he told himself. This time he would be the one to set the pace.

But inevitably, he lost himself in Katie. The more he tried to take from her, the more he felt him giving of himself. She threw her head back and opened herself to him, yet he was the one who surrendered. Deeper and deeper, he drove himself inside her, barely aware of how much of himself he was leaving behind. He pummeled her relentlessly. She crowded herself closer to him. In a frenzy of uncontrolled need, he exploded inside her. But Katie was the one to cry out at the culmination, as if his loss were giving her life.

It was a long moment before Cooper remembered who or where he was. When he did, it was to find Katie still lying beneath him, gasping for breath as if her lungs had been empty for some time. Only then did he remember to breathe, and when he did, his respiration was as erratic and frantic as her own.

The cry of a baby prevented him from speaking a word. Which was just as well, he thought. Because he had no idea what to say.

Evidently, Katie didn't, either, because she scrambled out from beneath him, grabbed for her shirt, and shrugged into it as she rushed toward the bedroom. Then she closed the door firmly behind herself. Cooper watched her go, his mind still reeling, his body still a mass of raw nerves.

And he wondered what the hell he was supposed to do now.

Nine

Cooper had always hated the whole morning-after thing. That's why he'd always avoided it by never spending the night with a woman. But that was going to be difficult with Katie, seeing as how she was pretty much living with him. Unless he moved out of his own apartment—or else asked her and her son to hit the bricks, which was even less likely—there was little chance he was going to be able to put off facing up to what had happened between them the night before.

Now as he stood in his kitchen sipping his morning coffee, he rehearsed in his head all the excuses, explanations and exhortations he was going to give Katie to minimize their...

Their what? he wondered. What was a good word for what the two of them had engaged in the night before? Their lovemaking? No, that suggested that love had actually been involved, and Cooper knew that wasn't the case at all. Their sexual encounter? Much more to the point, and certainly more accurate, but still not quite right. He'd had sex before, and it hadn't been anything like what he'd done with Katie.

So what exactly had he done with Katie? he asked himself again. What exactly was it that the two of them had shared last night? How was he going to describe their... their... their... impromptu. Yeah, that was it. Their *impromptu*. He wasn't sure what it meant exactly, but he'd heard the word in a movie. It was as good as any, he decided. It sounded exotic, sensual and temporary. It would be just the thing.

He topped off his coffee and exited the kitchen, just as Katie was about to enter it. Sweeping the cup of hot liquid back quickly, because she was carrying the baby, he moved out of her way, only to have her push past him as if he weren't there. He gave her a moment to retrieve whatever it was she needed, and when she returned to the living room with a big glass of orange juice, striding past him again as if he were invisible, Cooper stopped her with a word.

"Katie."

Immediately she halted, and spun around to face him. Before he could tell her anything more, however, she said, "I want to talk to an attorney."

It was, quite possibly, the last thing he expected to hear, under the circumstances. "A... an attorney?" he sputtered. "Hey, Katie, I know what happened last night wasn't something either of us planned, but do you really think a lawsuit is going to make it any better?"

She gazed at him for a moment, looking more than a little puzzled, more than a little hurt. Then she shook her head slowly. "No, I meant I want to talk to an attorney about Andy. About keeping custody of him. To see if maybe there's some chance I could actually keep William away from him, legally, physically and permanently. You're right in that I should talk to a lawyer about that, at least once. One session wouldn't cost that much, right?"

Cooper hesitated for a telling second before replying, "Oh. Right."

She spun around again and moved toward the sofa. "As far as I'm concerned, last night never happened. It was nothing more than a dream."

He followed her, taking a seat at the other end of the couch, placing as much space between them as he could. Without looking at her, he asked, "Been having dreams like that a lot lately, have you?"

She said nothing in response, simply settled the baby in her lap and sipped her juice.

Cooper sighed heavily. "Yeah, me, too."

"I'd rather not talk about it, okay?"

"Okay."

"I'd rather just put it down to both of us being a little emotionally strung out and a lot physically exhausted. Okay?"

"Okay."

"I'd rather just pretend it never happened. Okay?"

This time Cooper was the one to say nothing.

Katie turned her head to stare at him fully. "Okay?" she demanded again.

He stared down into his coffee, as if he might find the answer he sought there. Finally, he said, "Okay."

He knew he was lying, but he didn't care. There was no way he could pretend what had happened last night hadn't happened at all. And, all modesty aside, he suspected Katie couldn't, either. But he agreed that it would probably be best if neither of them said another word about it. She was right about one thing. They had been strung out emotionally, and they had been exhausted physically. Tensions ran high when two people were living in close, uncertain quarters, the way he and Katie had been for the last week. Naturally, eventually, the two of them were bound to succumb to extreme, and unexpected, behavior.

"My life's a wreck right now," she continued, sounding as if the words were drawn from her unwillingly. "The last thing I need...the last thing either one of us needs is..." She stopped abruptly and glanced down at the baby wiggling in her arms. "Do you know any lawyers?" she asked suddenly, clearly striving to put the other matter aside completely.

Cooper thought for a moment. "Yeah, a couple. Not real well, though. And I don't know if they handle stuff like custody or not. Personal injury, sure, but family matters..."

"Do you have their numbers?"

"I think so."

"It's a start." She said nothing for a moment, obviously lost in thought and the making of plans. Then she asked, "Do you have to work today?"

He shook his head. "As a matter of fact, I don't. Why?"

Her expression became somewhat anxious. "Would you mind baby-sitting for Andy for a little while?"

Actually, Cooper minded a lot. He'd never baby-sat before. Nor did he have any desire to do so now. He had no idea what a baby's needs were. Even though he'd spent the last week fascinated by Katie's care of her son—the baths she gave him in the dishpan, the way she blew raspberries on his tummy every time she changed his diaper, the gentle strokes of her fingertips along his arms and legs and back as the baby cooed his delight, the show tunes she sang while rocking him to sleep... Although Cooper found all those things unfathomable and foreign, he'd been drawn to them in a way he simply could not understand.

But that didn't mean he wanted to undertake the care and feeding of Andy himself. On the contrary. The more distance he kept from the little guy, the better. He had no desire to explore or exercise what questionable paternal activity might be present in his brain. He'd learned from example just how badly such instincts could go awry. His own father had been a bully and a brute. And although Cooper liked to think that being on the receiving end of violence throughout his childhood made him that much more determined that he would *never* wreak such malevolence on a child, he couldn't quite assure himself that that was the case at all.

"I, um . . ." he began.

"It would only be for a little while," Katie assured him.

"I don't think—"

"And it would be a lot easier for me to explain my situation to an attorney if I wasn't distracted by Andy."

"But—"

"Please, Cooper?"

He opened his mouth to tell her no, but heard himself say instead, "All right."

She smiled. "Thanks."

Reluctantly, he dropped his gaze to the infant tucked protectively in her arms. Andy stared back at him with an intensity that made Cooper want to squirm. It was as if those huge, blue-gray eyes could see right into the depths of his soul, as if Andy could tell by looking at him exactly what Cooper was capable of doing.

Then the baby smiled, a wide, gummy, toothless smile, and Cooper felt as if he'd just been exonerated after being unjustly accused of the most heinous crime. That small gesture of approval on Andy's part made him feel as if he were the most perfect human being alive. And he couldn't help but smile back.

"I'll just take a quick shower," he heard Katie say a bit breathlessly. "If that's okay."

"Sure," he told her, feeling a little distracted for some reason. "Don't worry about us. Andy and I will be just fine."

"Well, I have to tell you, Ms. Brennan, that I find your story to be more than a little incredible."

Katie stared at Lewis Prentiss, Esquire, and knew she wa
in trouble. The attorney in Mount Laurel wasn't one of the
ones Cooper had recommended, because, just as Cooper
had told her, all of them had specialized in personal injury
So Katie had done some sleuthing by herself in the Yellow
Pages and The Donnelly Directory, and had made a list of
her own. Lewis Prentiss had been at the top of that list. But
she was beginning to wonder if maybe in consulting him, she
had hit rock bottom. There was just something about the
guy that made her feel uneasy.

"I know it sounds hard to believe," she said. "But I as
sure you it happened exactly as I've told you."

"Perhaps if you gave me a few more details."

Details were the one thing that Katie had consciously
omitted from her story. She didn't want to reveal any more
than she had to—especially William's identity—unless she
knew she could trust whomever she decided to take on. *I*
she decided to take someone on. Still, this Prentiss guy wa
in New Jersey, she reminded herself, and not Philadelphia
Even though William was a fairly prominent person in the
City of Brotherly Love, there was a good chance he wa
fairly anonymous in South Jersey, which, in spite of being
just across the river, was a group of self-sufficient commu
nities that pretty much kept to themselves.

There was really no reason for her to distrust this man
but she did. She supposed the way she had been living for
the last two months made it impossible for her to place her
faith in anyone completely. Except Cooper, of course. For
some reason, she'd had no trouble at all trusting him.

And look what had happened there, a little voice inside
her head taunted her.

Just what on earth had she been thinking to let things go
as far as they had between the two of them the night be
fore? Wasn't it enough that her life was already a mess
Wasn't it enough that she had no idea where she was going
or what she should do? Wasn't it enough that she just barely

trusted herself lately, let alone someone she'd only known a matter of days? Why had she thrown yet another wrench into the works by making love with Cooper? What had she been thinking? Had she even been thinking at all?

They hadn't even used any protection, she berated herself further. Even though breastfeeding was supposed to offset the possibility of conception, it was by no means a sure thing.

She pushed the unhappy thoughts away and tried to focus again on the attorney seated on the other side of the desk. "I'd rather not discuss the details," she said, declining his request for more information. "Not yet anyway. I just want to know what my rights are. I just want to know if I have a halfway solid case against this man."

The attorney studied her in silence for a moment. "You say there's no record of your marriage in Las Vegas?"

She shook her head. "No. Apparently not."

"But the man is definitely the father of your child. A genetic test could prove that beyond a doubt?"

"Yes."

Lewis Prentiss steepled his fingers and gazed blandly at Katie from over them. "Then I'd say he does indeed have a leg to stand on. Of course, it would depend on the judge, and I'm sure there's more to the story that you haven't told me that would be significant, but from what you've said here so far..." He sighed and leaned forward. "Ms. Brennan, I'll be honest with you. It sounds to me as if there's a good chance this man might win custody of your son."

She'd told the lawyer nothing about naming Cooper as Andy's father on the birth certificate. It had been one of those details she'd thought best left unsaid. She bit her lip now to keep the revelation from tumbling out. For some reason, it seemed important that she say nothing more about it.

"Even if the man lied to me?" she asked. "Even if the man committed bigamy?"

"Unless there's a record of your marriage, there's no proof he's a bigamist. There's no evidence that he lied to you, either."

"There's my word," Katie said, the assurance sounding weak, even to her own ears.

"And there's his word," Mr. Prentiss added unnecessarily. "The question is, which will the judge believe?"

Katie sighed. She could pretty well answer that one herself. William would show up in court wearing one of his very expensive, beautifully tailored, pin-striped suits. He'd talk about his position as the executive vice president of a nationally respected chemical manufacturing company. He'd list his community activities, describe his involvement with the church, list the positions he held on cultural committees.

Then Katie would take the stand, wearing a dress she bought from a discount store, and would tell the judge that she had no job, no family, no money and no prospects. But, she would add fervently, she loved her son more deeply and could care for him more completely than any other human being could.

It would be the truth. And it wouldn't be nearly enough.

"Thank you for your time, Mr. Prentiss," she said gloomily. "You've been very helpful."

"Ms. Brennan, please. If you could just give me more to go on—"

"No, that's okay. I'm pretty sure I know my rights now." *Or rather, my lack of them,* she added morosely to herself.

"Well, do leave your address and telephone number with my secretary on your way out. I'll do some research and see if there's some precedent I've overlooked. I'll call you if I find out anything."

Katie nodded, but knew she wouldn't leave her address and phone number for the guy. It was probably bad enough that she'd given him her real name. For one thing, she still didn't trust him. For another, she just didn't see much point

The more she considered her situation, the more hopeless it became. And the more she wanted to turn to Cooper, to hold him close and bury her face in the warm skin of his neck, as he rocked her and murmured that everything was going to work out fine.

God, what a mess she'd made of her life.

Outside Lewis Prentiss's office, the day was clear, the sun was bright, and the sky was bluer than Katie had ever seen. She inhaled deeply of the warm afternoon, thinking that on such a day, she should be outdoors with her son, running through a field of flowers, introducing him to the joys of nature. Instead, Andy was locked up tight in Cooper's apartment, missing out on a breeze redolent of summer, on white clouds chasing after each other against a backdrop of azure, and on the song of a purple finch that chanted happily somewhere close by.

Until now, Katie didn't realize that she'd been missing out on such things, too. Even before she'd gone into hiding with her son, she had ceased to enjoy the most basic pleasures of life, even those that were available to her free of charge. When was the last time she had just taken a leisurely walk by herself? When was the last time she had looked at or for anything beyond what she had set out specifically to seek? When was the last time she had just sat back and let life happen to her, instead of struggling to carve one out for herself?

Not since she was a child, she realized now. And now that she had a child of her own, shouldn't she strive to make sure those experiences never went overlooked again? Shouldn't she go out of her way to make sure her son enjoyed his childhood as well as any child could? Andy had brought so many things to Katie's life that had been absent before. Things that she could never have conceived of, things that made what she had once thought so important, so all-consuming, seem silly somehow. She wanted to be sure

Andy grew up with an understanding of what was truly important in life.

And for some reason, out of nowhere, she wanted to be sure Cooper understood all that, too.

She wished she could share with him all the things that Andy had given to her. But how could she, when those things were completely intangible and utterly indescribable? She could try to tell Cooper about the intense sense of well-being she experienced every time Andy smiled at her. She could try to explain the sensation of unity she enjoyed every time she put her baby to her breast. She could try to put into suitable words how satisfied she felt every time she thought of her son as an adult part of the world.

But there was just so much to say, so many things to describe, such an overwhelming amount of emotion involved in those seemingly simple tasks. Was it even possible for Cooper to understand?

Katie found her way back to her bus stop feeling weighted down somehow. Automatically, she stepped aboard when the New Jersey Transit bus wheezed to a halt in front of her. Without thinking, she dropped the proper change into the fare box and took a seat halfway toward the back of the bus. Blindly, she watched the trees and houses and traffic pass by outside the filmy window.

And she wondered how on earth she was going to offer her son a life of simple pleasures and easy joy when she would be looking over her shoulder every step of the way.

Cooper stretched out alongside a sleeping Andy, watching the steady rise and fall of the baby's back as he breathed. Until Katie and her son had shown up at his front door, he couldn't remember the last time he'd lain on the floor, unless he was doing something of an intimate nature with someone of the opposite sex. But since the arrival of his guests, Cooper had been lying on the floor a lot. And only once had that thing with the opposite sex been involved.

It was a whole different world from down here, he thought, one that gave a man an entirely different perspective on things. He glanced over at the legs of the only chair in the living room, and thought they looked like a series of cross beams laid out for a new building. A spider crawled slowly up one, paused for a moment, lifted a leg as if in greeting, then disappeared on the other side. Cooper noted a dark splotch on the rug to his left that he hadn't noticed before and made a mental note to rent one of those steam cleaners. And over there in the corner, between the stereo cabinet and the sofa, was the Robbie Robertson tape that had been missing for more than a year.

"Well, I'll be damned," he muttered to himself. "It really *is* a whole different world from down here."

It must be kind of tough being a baby, he thought, returning his attention to the quietly slumbering Andy. To be nothing but a bundle of sensual awareness and unlimited potential, yet have no concept of the nature of reality. You had no way to let people know what you had on your mind except by squalling and smiling and hoping that your diaper was fragrant enough that someone might think to put a clean one on you at some point during the day. You got stuck with a bland diet, a limited wardrobe, no mode of self-supported transportation, and very little opportunity for meaningful conversation. Not exactly a great way to live.

In spite of that, Andy seemed to be a pretty happy little guy. When he was awake, anyway. Cooper noted, not for the first time, that newborns sure did do a lot of sleeping. Except at night, of course. At night, he thought he heard Katie up and around a half-dozen times, at least. There had been occasions when he'd come close to knocking on the bedroom door to see if there was anything he could do to help her out. Then he'd reminded himself that she was feeding her son, an activity that pretty much required absolutely no assistance from him.

Katie could take care of her kid just fine without him, Cooper told himself. Hell, she'd been doing just that for two months, hadn't she? Just because he still had this stupid, unexplainable feeling that he was the one who should be looking out for both of them... That didn't mean anything, right? That didn't mean he should do whatever he had to do to be sure they were safe, right? That didn't mean he should actually accept responsibility for the two of them, right?

"Yo, Andy," he said softly to the sleeping baby. "We really ought to talk about your situation here."

The infant's eyes remained steadfastly shut, but his lips parted fractionally, as if he wanted to respond, but simply lacked the proper vocal skills to manage it.

"Your mom and you," Cooper went on, "you need to see about getting yourselves out of trouble. This arrangement we've got going now... it's just not working at all."

The baby inhaled two quick breaths, released them slowly, and made a smacking noise with his lips.

"I mean it, Andy," Cooper continued quietly. "You and your mom are great and all that, but... the way things are going here now, you're not exactly conducive to a normal routine. Know what I mean? Something's going to have to give."

Andy uttered an almost silent sound that Cooper could have sworn was an agreement.

"So what are we going to do about it, pal?" he asked further. "Just out of curiosity, what's *your* take on this whole thing?"

Andy's eyes drifted open, and he met Cooper's gaze with a steely intent. For a split second, Cooper thought the baby was trying to tell him something, and halfway expected the little guy to articulate a thoughtful answer to his question. Then Andy smiled, and a small stream of spittle dripped from the side of his mouth. Cooper couldn't help but chuckle.

"Drivel," he said to the baby. "Yeah, a lot of people say the same thing about my conversational skills. Okay, you win. We'll do whatever you want to do. So name it."

But Andy didn't reply right away. Instead, he just stared at Cooper as if to say, "Yeah, right. I can't even roll over on my own yet, you jerk. It's *your* job to entertain me."

Cooper was about to push himself up off the floor and move the baby to the kitchen, where Andy would at least have a change of scenery while Cooper fixed himself lunch, when the sound of a key scraped in the front door, followed immediately by Katie's appearance on the other side.

"Hi," she said softly when she closed the door behind her.

Cooper rolled to his stomach and settled his chin on his hands. "Hi. How did it go?"

"Not so hot."

She moved to the sofa and slumped onto it. With much maneuvering, Andy turned his head to the side so that he could see his mother, then wriggled with delight at the sight of her. Katie laughed and immediately moved to the floor, dropping a heartfelt kiss onto the crown of the baby's head before seating herself cross-legged on carpet near him. She splayed her fingers open over Andy's back, as if she drew life from his warmth and activity. Cooper supposed that in many ways, she did.

"I found a guy in Mount Laurel named Lewis Prentiss who handles custody cases," she said, looking at the baby instead of Cooper. "I didn't tell him a lot about my situation, but I hit the high points. And with things the way they are between me and William, Prentiss thinks that if we did go to court over Andy, there's a good chance William would win."

Cooper took a moment to digest that, then said, "But he's not positive that would happen, right?"

She shook her head. "No. I guess nothing's one hundred percent guaranteed. But he's of the opinion that there's a backlash against single mothers in some parts of the country right now—this one included—and if I landed in court with the wrong judge, I might find myself being made an example to other potential single mothers.''

Cooper nodded, but said nothing.

Katie stared at her son, her face ravaged by devastation. "I can't lose him, Cooper. I couldn't live if I lost Andy. It would be like losing a part of myself. I wish I could explain it better. I wish I could make you understand. But unless you've been a parent yourself, unless you know what it's like to..."

Her voice drifted off, and Cooper was grateful for it. He didn't need to be reminded that he was incapable of feeling a positive emotion like the love one might embrace for a child. The potential for that had fairly well been beaten out of him when he was a child himself. To hear Katie reiterate the sentiment now just made it that much more difficult for him to stomach. So, as he always did when such a situation arose, he tried not to let it get to him.

"No one says you have to lose Andy," he told her. "You've only talked to one lawyer. You'll just consult a couple more, that's all."

She shook her head again, her dark hair falling forward to partially obscure her face. "No. They'll all tell me the same thing. This guy obviously knew what he was talking about. Andy and I are..." She sighed, leaving the statement unfinished.

She rubbed her hand lightly over the baby's back in a slow circle, bent her head toward his, and lowered her voice when she spoke again, her words clearly intended for her son alone. "I'm sorry, sweetie, but I'm not going to be able to give you all the things I'd like to give you. You're not going to have the greatest childhood in the world, because we'll never be able to stop looking back. But I'll love you with all my heart. As long as I'm alive, you'll always have that. I promise you.''

It was a promise Cooper found himself wishing Katie would make to him. Then as soon as the thought formed in his head, he shoved it away hard. The last thing he needed or wanted was a promise of something for forever. Forever was way too long to have anything. Who the hell knew what time did to things?

"Katie," he said softly.

She snapped her head up to look at him, her expression one that indicated she had forgotten she and her son weren't alone. "What?" she asked, the one-word response sounding more like a sigh.

"You can't do this."

She looked puzzled. "Do what?"

"You can't keep running away from Andy's father the way you have been."

"Why not?"

"Because it's no way to live, that's why."

She expelled a disgusted sound. "I know that. But what other choice do I have?"

Cooper hesitated a long time before he answered her question, trying to talk himself out of describing what, for all intents and purposes, seemed like a perfectly good alternative. It was wrong, he told himself. It was a violation of the rights of another human being, however monstrous that human being might be. There was a very good chance it might even be illegal. It would be stupid and suicidal to set himself up the way he was about to set himself up.

Nevertheless, he said, "You do have another choice, Katie."

"Yeah, I could go to court and risk losing Andy forever."

"No, I mean other than that. You have another choice."

She eyed him warily. "What is it?"

Cooper sighed quickly, halfheartedly, then spit out the words as quickly as he could, so that they almost sounded like one. "You could let Andy's father be responsible for him."

"Andy's father..." Her expression changed from wary to utterly confused. "I thought we *were* talking about Andy's father. What are you talking about? William is—"

"William *claims* to be his father," Cooper said. "I'm talking about Andy's legal father—the one whose name is on his birth certificate.

"Me," he clarified when she still showed no sign of understanding. "You could let me be responsible for Andy."

Ten

_____

"You?"

Katie told herself she must have misunderstood. Cooper couldn't possibly be offering to do what he was offering to do. Why would he? Why would any man accept responsibility for a child who wasn't his?

But he met her gaze levelly, and replied in a voice that was anything but uncertain, "Yeah. Me. I'm Andy's rightful father after all, aren't I? It says so right on his birth certificate."

"But—"

"Katie, it's the only way you're going to be able to keep custody of your son without the risk of losing him. You and I could get married—"

"Married?"

"Yeah, married. That would give you everything you don't have now that a judge would consider so important—relatives, roots, a home, an income...a way to support

Andy, the perfect environment to raise him in. You'd give him a legal, legitimate, full-time father."

He grinned mischievously before adding, "Maybe, if we put our heads together, we can even come up with a decent story to counter Winslow's claim of paternity and cast aspersions on his character. Granted, we'd be perjuring ourselves if it went as far as court, but it would be for a good cause."

When Katie remained silent, he sat up and scooted himself over beside her. He draped an arm around her shoulder, pulled her close and squeezed hard.

"Even if something does happen to prove that Winslow is Andy's biological father, at least being married to me would give you some leverage. You'd be able to offer Andy a future every bit as stable as the one Winslow could. Middle class instead of upper class, but still... Maybe, just maybe, simply by virtue of being the boy's mother, you'd win custody. So why don't you...you know...marry me?"

Well, that certainly was effective at making her speechless. Katie honestly didn't think there had ever been a time in her life when she hadn't known what to say, but Cooper's proposal accomplished that with no trouble at all.

He qualified his offer immediately by adding, "At least long enough to let Winslow know that he doesn't have a claim on Andy. Let the bastard find another brood mare."

Katie shook her head vehemently, choosing to focus on the second part of Cooper's statement, because the first part—the part about him only wanting to be married to her as long as it took to establish Andy's legitimacy—was just too troubling to consider.

"No, that's something else, Cooper. I have to make sure William doesn't try something like this again. Because he's just crazy enough to do it. Only the next time he does it, he might not be as nice to the woman he goes after as he was to me."

"Nice," Cooper repeated. "You think this guy was nice to you?"

"Compared to what could have happened in this situation, and after seeing the way he beat up his wife? Yeah. You bet I do. I don't even want to think about what he'd resort to in his desperation next time."

She could see that Cooper was about to say more, but he checked himself. Instead, he asked her, "So, what do you say? Will you marry me?"

"Absolutely not."

He gazed at her blankly for a moment, and she couldn't for the life of her tell what he was thinking. "That was awfully quick," he said quietly, his voice surprisingly void of any emotion. "You want to reconsider?"

"No," she told him. "There's no need to reconsider. There's no way I'm going to wreck your life any worse than I already have. It's bad enough that Andy and I have cramped your style for a week, and that it will probably take months for me to undo a legal wrong where his birth certificate is concerned. I refuse to make matters any worse than they already are."

"Katie—"

"I said, no, Cooper, and that's final. It was nice of you to offer, but . . . no."

He obviously hadn't thought this through at all, Katie told herself. He couldn't possibly have considered all the repercussions of what it would mean to marry her and accept Andy as his own son. An arrangement like that would serve to tie the two of them—the three of them—together forever, regardless of how long their farce of a marriage lasted.

And that was another thing. How could Katie marry Cooper, feeling the way she did about him? When she didn't even *know* how she felt about him? How could she know, when her emotions had been on overload for the last two months? There had actually been times this week when she'd fancied herself in love with him. Last night, when the two of them had made love, for one brief moment, she'd even allowed herself to think that maybe he loved her, too.

What a laugh. What a joke. What a jerk she was.

She'd fallen hard, fast, for one man, and she'd wound up on the run, trying to protect her child as a result. How was she supposed to trust her feelings for Cooper? At best, what she felt for him was probably nothing more than gratitude. At worst, it was some strange, temporary, postpartum hormonal reaction that made her think she loved him.

In either case, if she married him, it would be no time at all before she came to her senses and realized what a terrible mistake she'd made. Or maybe Cooper would be the one to come to that conclusion first and walk out on her. And then she'd be riding that roller coaster of emotion again, headed right into a downward spiral.

Nope. No way. She wasn't about to open herself up for something like that again. Cooper was being sweet. But he wasn't being realistic. Thank God one of them, anyway, had the presence of mind to realize that.

"Andy and I will be leaving tomorrow," Katie said as she stood, scooping the baby up with her.

Cooper stared at her openmouthed and incredulous looking. "What? Tomorrow? Why?"

If she hadn't known better, she would have sworn he sounded disappointed instead of relieved.

"Because we've overstayed our welcome," she told him. "And because that lawyer I saw just gave me the creeps for some reason. I think Andy and I need to be moving on."

Cooper stood, too, settling his hands on his hips in a gesture that was unquestionably challenging. "Moving on where?" he asked. "You don't have any place to go."

She lifted one shoulder in a halfhearted shrug. "I don't know," she told him honestly. "But I didn't know where I was going the first time, either, and Andy and I did okay."

He expelled a single, humorless chuckle. "Katie, when you showed up at my front door, you were half-dead from exhaustion and frightened out of your wits. I wouldn't call that 'okay.'"

"We'll be fine this time."

"I don't think it's a good idea."

"It doesn't matter what you think, Cooper. You're not responsible for us."

Without waiting for him to comment further, Katie retreated to the bedroom and collapsed beside her son on the bed. Only then did she realize how fast her heart was beating. Only then did she realize how empty of air her lungs had become. She gulped in a few quick gasps of breath, then closed her eyes and willed her pulse rate to slow.

What bothered her most wasn't that Cooper had just offered to lie for her in a court of law. What bothered her most wasn't that she had completely run out of options. What bothered her most wasn't even that a villain might, at that very moment, be closing in on the location where she was hiding her son.

No, what bothered Katie most was that she had wanted so desperately to take Cooper up on his proposal of marriage. Whether he loved her or not. Whether he needed her or not. For as long as the tenuous arrangement would last.

She'd been a sucker for a man once, she reminded herself. She'd thought someone loved her enough to make her his forever. And unlike her phony husband, Cooper hadn't even mentioned the word *love*. Nor had he said anything about forever.

At least he was honest, she told herself. But the realization brought little comfort.

Cooper stared at his bedroom door for a long time, trying to tell himself he had not done what he'd just done. Had he actually just offered to commit perjury, and for the welfare of a child, no less? Had he actually just asked Katie to marry him? Had he actually just suggested that she make her son—a child who had come into his life by sheer, dumb luck—his son, too, in the eyes of the law and for the world at large?

Had he actually just been hurt when she'd turned down his proposal?

Nah. Couldn't be.

He just hadn't been getting nearly enough sleep since Katie and Andy invaded his life, that's all. He spun around, drove two big hands through his hair and told himself to get a grip.

One thing was certain, though, he thought. His life was never going to go back to its dubious normalcy until Katie and her son got their lives straightened out. And if she took off tomorrow, it would make matters worse, not better. As if he wasn't already losing enough sleep, worrying about their fate as they faced the world alone would keep him awake nights more surely than anything else would.

He moved slowly to the bedroom door and rapped lightly three times.

"Yes?" Katie called out from the other side.

"Can we talk about this some more?" he asked.

"Not now. I'm feeding Andy."

He expelled a sigh of exasperation. "Then when?"

He heard nothing for a moment, then she told him, "I think we've said everything we need to say."

"And I think you're wrong about that," he replied.

"Cooper, just let it go, please."

"Not yet. Promise me you and Andy won't go anywhere until I check out one more thing I need to check out."

"What's that?"

Cooper wondered how much he should tell her, then decided to tell her nothing at all. He didn't want to get her hopes up, didn't want to see her dejection if the avenue he was about to travel down wound up being a dead end.

What he was planning to do was a shot in the dark at best. But it might lead to something that could help them out. Cooper may not have a lot of friends, but he had a large number of acquaintances, lawyers just being the tip of the iceberg. It might not hurt to put a few bugs in a few ears, just to see what developed.

"I have to go out for a while," he said quickly. "I don't know when I'll be back. Don't wait up."

When she offered no indication that she'd heard him, he called out more loudly, "Katie?"

"Okay, I won't wait up."

"And promise me you and Andy won't go anywhere just yet."

Only a small hesitation, but one Cooper didn't like, followed by her softly uttered, "Okay."

"Promise me."

"I promise."

"Say, 'Cooper, I promise Andy and I won't go anywhere until after you get back from running your errand.'"

He heard an exasperated sigh, followed by "Cooper, I promise Andy and I won't go anywhere until after you get back from running your errand."

Her vow wasn't as reassuring as he had hoped, but for Cooper, for now, it was enough. It was going to have to be.

Katie was asleep when he returned home, but Andy wasn't. As Cooper closed the front door quietly behind him at just past midnight, he heard the soft cooing of the infant who lay, as always, in the middle of the living room floor. His mother lay on the rug beside him, fast asleep, and Cooper could see that the exhaustion of the last two months and the stress of the last several days had finally overtaken her. Had it not been for the heavy rise and fall of her back as she inhaled and exhaled, he would have thought she was dead.

With all the gentleness and care of an artist handling his work, Cooper lifted Katie easily into his arms and carried her into the bedroom, settling her on her back on the same side of the bed he occupied himself when he was alone. Vaguely, he noted that the bedclothes carried the faint scent of her, and he wondered how long the fragrance would remain after she left his life for good. Hopefully, for a long, long time, he thought. But then, he already knew that whatever Katie left behind would stay with him forever, whether he wanted those remnants of her to linger or not.

He returned to the living room to retrieve Andy, too, scooping up the baby as effortlessly as he had Katie only a moment ago. The tiny body squirmed against him, warm and lively and redolent of that soft aroma that is distinctly baby in nature. Until he'd held Andy for the first time, Cooper had never realized babies had a particular smell. Nor had he realized how soft and warm they were. Nor had it occurred to him just how delicate, and yet sturdy, they could be.

He literally held life in his hands when he hugged Andy to his chest, he thought as he carried the baby into the bedroom to join his mother. But what that life would become was almost entirely up to the person who held the greatest influence over him. If everything worked out the way it was supposed to, that influence would be Katie. It would be love, warmth, generosity and open-mindedness.

Unfortunately, Cooper thought further as he fumbled to close the tabs of the dry diaper he'd slipped onto the tiny body, then settled his own great bulk into the spindly rocking chair, the world didn't always work the way it was supposed to.

Cooper pushed the rocking chair back and forth with both feet flat on the floor, trying to rock Andy to sleep. He wasn't sure exactly how to go about soothing a wide-awake child, but then, he hadn't had a clue how to change a diaper until a few days ago, either, and he was doing all right with that particular chore. It amazed him still how worldly he had considered himself before the night the snowstorm had blown him into Katie and Andy's lives. But until the baby's birth, Cooper realized now, he'd known nothing of what was truly important in life.

Hell, until he'd seen the look on Katie's face that afternoon, after the prospect of losing her son had fully registered on her, Cooper hadn't comprehended just what it meant to love a child. But Katie's fear had been palpable, and very nearly overwhelming. And somehow, she had transferred that fear to Cooper. He, too, had suddenly begun to halfway understand what a great, gaping hole Andy's loss would open in her soul. Cooper understood, because he began to feel it himself.

He turned his head to observe the still squiggling Andy, who likewise turned his head to gaze at Cooper. It wasn't fair, he thought, that a child who emerged from the womb so innocent and loving could be so easily tainted by the wrong kind of upbringing. What if Winslow did win custody of Andy? The same child Cooper held now, the one he envisioned doing nothing but good, being nothing but decent, as an adult, might very well wind up ruthless, thoughtless and careless, just like his biological father.

In the scant light of the bedroom, Cooper studied the baby in his arms, who stared back at him unblinking. There was no way in hell he would ever let someone turn Andy into that kind of creature. No way.

No way.

He shifted the infant to his shoulder and began the back-and-forth movement of the rocking chair again. He felt Andy's warm breath on his neck, felt the baby's tiny heart beating steadily just above his own. Life. So simple. How could Cooper not have seen it before?

The baby squirmed again, fighting sleep, so Cooper began to hum. He didn't know any songs by Gershwin, but he knew a lot by Sam Cooke. He closed his eyes, and in a low, easy baritone, he began to sing. He told Andy all about what it was like to have another Saturday night, but to have nobody.

By the time he finished the second chorus, the infant was fast asleep. But Cooper kept singing, just for good measure, and because he hated to see anything go unfinished. His eyes were still closed, and his palm was cupped firmly under the baby's bottom. He marveled again at how little the tiny human being weighed. Someday Andy might be as big as Cooper was. But for now, he was scarcely larger or sturdier than a sack of flour.

When he finished the song, Cooper opened his eyes and moved to get up out of the rocking chair. He had intended to place the baby in bed beside his slumbering mother. Only when Cooper looked up did he realize that Katie was awake, and evidently had been for some time. She sat at the head of his bed with her legs drawn up in front of her, her arms wrapped fiercely about her knees. And all Cooper could do was think about how badly he wanted to make love to her.

Without acknowledging that he'd just been caught in a moment he would rather not have had anyone witness, he stood and carried the baby back out into the living room, placing Andy on his stomach on the quilt that still lay open on the floor. Then he went back into the bedroom, pulling the door closed behind him until it was barely ajar. He trained his gaze steadily on Katie as he approached her, but said nothing when he joined her on the bed. Instead, he pulled her toward himself, folded his arms over her back, and kissed her.

It wasn't the searing, demanding kiss he had envisioned it would be. Instead, he brushed his lips lightly over hers, once, twice, three times, before dipping his head to the warm skin of her throat. He tangled his fingers in the hair above her nape, tipping her head back so that he had better access to the curve where her neck joined her shoulder. He pushed the soft fabric of her T-shirt aside, drew the tip of his tongue across the length of her collarbone, then covered her mouth with his again.

"Cooper," she whispered when she pulled away, "we can't do this. One time was a mistake. Two times would be—"

"Shh," he murmured, kissing her again. He moved his head away from hers long enough to add, "You're dreaming now. Just dreaming," then lowered it to claim her lips once more.

She kissed him back at length, her tongue joining his in a dance of sexual celebration. But again, she pulled away.

"I don't think this is a dream," she said softly. "My dreams have never felt this good before."

He nipped the skin of her shoulder with his teeth, then laved the small wound when she gasped. "Okay, so it's not a dream," he conceded.

"Cooper—"

"Shh," he murmured again. "I'm trying to get you to change your mind."

She sighed when he lifted his hand to cover her breast. "A-about what?" she stammered.

He closed and opened his hand over the warm flesh of her breast, flexing his fingers into the softness before raking his thumb back and forth across the aching peak. But he never answered her question.

"Oh," she murmured on a long sigh. "Oh, Cooper."

He dropped his hand to the hem of her shirt, and without asking, dragged the garment up over her head and tossed it to the floor. Then he reached behind her to unfasten her brassiere, and it, too, fell to the floor. He buried his head between her breasts, nuzzling their warmth, caressing their softness. He held one in each hand to tease, taunt, tickle and taste until Katie thought she would go mad with wanting.

Because it was madness to let this continue, she knew. But somehow, she could think of no way to stop it. Simply put, she didn't want to stop it. Making love with Cooper again was probably the stupidest, most self-destructive thing she could do. But it might also be the last opportunity she had to experience pure, unembellished joy.

Tomorrow, she and Andy would be leaving Cooper for good. Tonight, Katie wanted to simply love him for what felt like, at least momentarily, forever.

She curled her fingers in his hair and pulled him close, arching her back toward him to offer him freer access of the prize he so clearly wanted to plunder. He opened his mouth over the top of her breast, suckling and laving the skin with his tongue until a perfect circle pinkened her flesh where his mouth had been. His fingers glided up and down her torso, strumming each rib as if playing the most exquisite celestial music on the most fragile of instruments.

Then she felt his hands at her waist, unfastening the closure of her jeans. Katie dropped her own hands to help him, skimming the rest of her clothes off and falling back on the bed until she lay beneath him naked. He moved his hand between their bodies, fumbling for the fastenings of his own clothes. But his actions only aroused Katie more, and she took his hand in her own, guiding it to that part of her that demanded much more thorough attention.

Eagerly, Cooper obliged her, burying his fingers in her warm, damp folds. His movements were slow, then quick, calculated and easy one minute, random and insistent the next. And gradually, so gradually Katie almost lost herself, his motions went completely out of control. She bucked and writhed beneath him, clinging to his wrist with both hands as if trying to imprison him where he was forever. And then she went still and rigid for a moment, to let one long shudder wind its way through her entire body. After that, she collapsed, hooking her legs over Cooper's, twining her fingers with his.

He was hard and heavy atop her. Katie could feel every inch of him pulsing with life, anxious to get on with it. For one more moment, she simply lay beneath him, loving his weight, his heat, his life. Then she let loose of his hands and, with trembling fingers, opened his shirt and trousers and pushed them both away.

Cooper moved away from her long enough to shed his clothing, then rejoined her on the bed. When Katie rolled away from him to grab the edge of the bedspread, intending to pull it down so the two of them would be more comfortable, Cooper fitted himself easily behind her. He pulled her close and reached around her, to open his hand over her abdomen.

"I'd love to put another baby inside of you," he whispered, his lips scarcely a hairbreadth from her ear. "To watch you grow big, to hear its first heartbeat, to watch it kick against your belly. I've witnessed birth, Katie. I'd like to witness life, too."

She opened her mouth to ask him what was the difference, and to ask why he would want to create a bond that would tie the two of them together forever. But he dipped his hand lower at the same time he moved his hips forward, and she was overcome by the mixture of sensations that assailed her inside and out. Cooper withdrew for a moment, then plunged inside her again, this time pushing both palms against her belly to pull her back against him.

After that, Katie could scarcely think at all. When Cooper entered her, it was as if she became an entirely new being. As if the union of two made them both more whole as one. Together, they scaled a peak in a rhythmic climb, finally reaching a pinnacle that brought both exquisite pleasure and achingly melancholy pain. Together, they climaxed, and they cried out as one.

Katie crashed first, letting her body fall back against the bed, feeling limp and satisfied as she murmured something unintelligible. Cooper lay beside her, his head propped on one elbow, watching for a long time as she slept. For the first time since he'd met her, she seemed to be completely untroubled. For the first time, she seemed to be at peace.

Cooper smiled. He knew how she felt.

Then he lay down beside her and gathered her close. He hooked his chin over her shoulder, curled both arms around her waist, and covered her legs with his.

Tomorrow, he thought, they could talk again. Tomorrow, he would offer up his proposal of marriage again. Tomorrow, he could be honest about wanting to keep Katie—and Andy—by his side forever. Tomorrow, surely, she would see that.

Tomorrow, he assured himself just before sleep claimed him, things would be different between them.

Katie was smiling when she woke up, and she understood why immediately. Cooper still lay behind her, holding her close, his warm breath making the curls above her ear dance, his heartbeat thumping in rhythmic contentment between her shoulder blades. Beyond the bedroom door, she heard the soft cooing of her son, a sound that let her know he was hungry, but not quite demanding breakfast yet. Outside, it was still dark. A warm, silent breeze nudged the metal blinds over the window just enough to make them sing a whisper-soft song.

A woman should wake up in such a way every morning, she thought. Maybe, someday, Katie would.

She eased herself away from Cooper, reluctant to wake him, but needing to see to her son. After pushing herself quietly away from the bed, she slipped on her panties and shrugged back into her T-shirt, then moved silently out to the living room. She lifted Andy into her arms and moved to the couch, then put the infant to her breast and closed her eyes.

Outside the open window, a car moved quietly past the building, and Katie recalled what it had been like to get up early and go to work. To hear the alarm erupt at 4:00 a.m., to leap from a bed she occupied alone, to throw on her waitress uniform while gulping her coffee, and to arrive at work by four-thirty for the relay race of the breakfast shift. She'd go home after the lunch crowd left, grab a quick nap, and return in time for the dinner rush. Day in and day out. And around and around again.

Her only companions in that life had been her co-workers and the regulars at the diner, and the stray tomcat who had come to the back entrance of the restaurant from time to time for a handout. No wonder she had seen William as her savior. No wonder she had succumbed to him so easily. No wonder she had always tamped down her suspicions about him, instead celebrating her sudden good fortune whenever those suspicions had arisen.

But that had been a long time ago, she thought now. A million years ago. At least, it seemed like a million years ago. So much had happened in scarcely twelve months' time.

She dozed off after she switched Andy to her other breast, and didn't awaken until another car passed outside. But this time, it didn't quite go past the apartment. This time, it sounded as if it stopped and the ignition shut off. Katie opened her eyes and gazed idly out the window.

Then her heart nearly stopped beating and she came wide awake.

A black Jaguar sat at the curb, its tinted windows reflecting back the hazy round circle of the street lamp above. It was a car exactly like the one William drove. No, not *like* the one he drove, she realized as a vicious heat ignited in her midsection. It *was* the one he drove. It was William's car. Katie would know it anywhere.

Andy had finished his breakfast and had fallen back to sleep in her arms, and Katie could only sit motionless, staring down at him. For one bleak moment, she had no idea what to do, no inkling of how to proceed. Then her brain

lurched into action. Unfortunately, all it could do was ask
questions.

How had William found her? Who had told him she was
here? What would he do once he saw Andy? She already
knew he was capable of violence—did that mean he would
hurt her? Hurt her son? Hurt Cooper?

Cooper.

The realization of what he had done hit Katie full force
then. Cooper must have been the one to tell William where
she was. Because no one else *knew* where she was. Even the
attorney who had made her feel so uneasy didn't know
where to find her. She'd covered her tracks well for months.
Until she'd come to Cooper. Then she'd let herself off the
hook. She'd let herself trust him to make sure she was safe.
She'd let him do the thinking for her.

She reminded herself how he'd shown up out of nowhere
the night Andy was born, completely unasked for. That had
been one weird coincidence. But she might have let it go at
coincidence if it wasn't for William's appearance now.
Cooper had told her he had to go somewhere last night,
right after she'd told him she was planning to leave today.

Had he gone to see William? she wondered. Had Cooper
simply been keeping an eye on her for the last week so that
William could make arrangements for claiming Andy? Had
all that ridiculous talk yesterday about marriage simply been
a stalling tactic to keep her under wraps until William could
tighten the noose around her neck?

Or was Cooper honestly trying to help her and Andy out?

She couldn't quite bring herself to believe he was working for William. In spite of the evidence right outside the
window, she tried to tell herself that Cooper had nothing to
do with her phony husband's appearance now. Cooper was
too nice, had been too attentive and too good to her and
Andy. Hadn't she just witnessed him singing her son to sleep
the night before? Hadn't he just made love to her in the

sweetest, most exquisite way? How could a man be so gentle and caring while committing the worst kind of deceit?

It was the same question she had asked herself about William on more than one occasion.

Katie didn't know for sure whether or not Cooper was guilty of doing what she suspected him of doing. But right now, she couldn't afford to trust her instincts or him. She had to think about Andy. Andy's welfare—and that alone—was what drove Katie now. She couldn't take any chances with her son's life. Probably, Cooper had nothing to do with William's appearance outside. Probably, Cooper was as blind to what her fake husband was planning as she was. Probably, Cooper wasn't the one who'd told William where to find her.

But possibly—maybe—he was.

As silently as she dared, Katie put Andy down and returned to Cooper's bedroom to collect her things. All the while, her heart pounded so fiercely, she feared it would wake him. And all the while, she forced back her tears. She allowed herself one final glimpse of him as he slept. His arms were still curled around an invisible object across the spot where she had lain beside him. His head was cradled by the pillow he had shared with her. He looked so innocent, so incapable of treachery.

But then, so had William.

Out in the living room, Katie slipped on a pair of blue jeans and tugged a sweatshirt on over her T-shirt. Then she fastened the Snugli around her waist, tucked her sleeping son inside, and covered both with a cotton blanket. Hoisting her duffel bag up over her shoulder with one hand, and curving the other protectively over her son's back, Katie crept to the kitchen and went out through the back door.

She hugged the shadows and walked until she was a mile or more from Cooper's apartment. Then she found an all-night diner and went inside. But only when she and Andy were tucked safely and obscurely in a high-backed booth in the corner of the room farthest from the entrance, did Katie allow herself to cry. Even then, however, she was unable to think about what she was going to do next.

Eleven

The ceaseless pounding finally registered in Cooper's brain, and he woke with a start.

"Katie?" he mumbled as he opened his eyes. His fingers curled convulsively over the sheet on the other side of the bed, gripping a handful of the cool, soft fabric.

But no warm, soft Katie.

Cooper relaxed his fist and shut his eyes again when he remembered that Katie wasn't there. She hadn't been for days. She had disappeared five mornings ago without a trace. Just like before. Just like that. He was beginning to wonder if he hadn't simply imagined her presence in his life both times.

Then he opened his eyes again and saw the rocking chair in the corner of his bedroom and was reminded once more that his time with Katie and her son had been all too real.

And all too temporary.

The rapping at his front door started up again, so Cooper pushed himself up and away from the bed. Cripes, it felt as if he'd just turned in, he thought as he tugged on a pair of well-worn jeans. He glanced at the clock on the nightstand to find that, in spite of it being just after 9:00 a.m., he had in fact been in bed less than an hour.

Since Katie's departure, he'd been switching his day shifts for nights at work. Somehow, it was easier to be alone in his apartment during the daylight hours than it was after dark. Plus, nights in the summer seemed busier for a paramedic for some reason, and having to keep his mind on his work prevented Cooper's thoughts from dwelling on memories of Katie and Andy.

"I'm coming!" he shouted out as he approached the front door, the fierce knocking showing no sign of ceasing. "What?" he then barked out when he yanked open the front door.

A very smarmy-looking individual stood on the other side, a man who, for some reason, seemed much smaller than he actually was. He had overly oiled hair and was wearing a well-cut suit that would have fit someone a little taller perfectly. All in all, he appeared to be a bit... unwholesome. For some reason, that was the only word Cooper could think of that seemed appropriate for him.

Wearily, Cooper raked a hand through his hair and sighed. "What?" he repeated with a little less vehemence. "What do you want?"

"I'm looking for Katherine Brennan," the man said.

"Yeah, well, so are a lot of other people," Cooper told him frankly. "Including me. What do you want with her?"

The man reached into his pocket and extracted a business card that he then thrust at Cooper. "I'm Lowell Madison. I'm an attorney for William Winslow. He's interested in locating his son."

Cooper pretended to study the card in his hand and told himself not to overreact. He didn't know how Winslow had made the connection between him and Katie, nor could he know for sure if this had anything to do with her disappearance. He took some comfort in reasoning that if Winslow had already found her, this lackey Madison wouldn't be standing at his front door. It didn't change the fact, however, that Katie was still missing from Cooper's life. Nor did it provide him with any more insight into her whereabouts.

Nor did it reassure him that she was safe.

Schooling his features into the blandest expression he could master, he glanced back up at the attorney and shrugged. "So?"

Lowell Madison eyed him warily. "So Ms. Brennan is the child's mother, and we have reason to believe you know the whereabouts of both of them."

Cooper sighed, then searched deep inside himself to draw on what little he could remember of his high school drama class, wishing like hell that he hadn't ditched school so often when he was a kid. Still, his teacher had told him at one point that he had some talent, if he'd just quit fighting and screwing up long enough to master it. Instead of listening, Cooper had taken a swing at his teacher. Fortunately, he'd missed the guy, but it had landed him with a suspension nonetheless. In spite of that, talent was talent, right? he reasoned. He only hoped it had stayed with him all these years.

He straightened and looked Lowell Madison squarely in the eye. "Look," he told the other man, "Katie has a son, yeah. But I'm the kid's father." He thrust the card back at the attorney. "I don't know who this William Winslow guy is, but... if he thinks Andy's his, he's mistaken. Sorry."

"But—"

"Anyway, it doesn't matter, because Katie took off with Andy a few days ago, and I don't know where she went."

Lowell Madison fingered his business card thoughtfully. He remained silent for several moments, his expression revealing nothing of what might be going on in his head. But his eyes never left Cooper's. Finally, he said, "She could be guilty of kidnapping then."

Cooper threw him a dismissive look. "It's her kid. How can she be napping him? Look, this has happened before. Katie and I get into an argument, she splits for a while—and now that we have Andy, she takes him along—then she comes home and we kiss and make up. Maybe we're not the greatest model of domestic bliss, but we do our best. Not that it's any of *your* business," he added meaningfully.

Madison looked thoughtful for a few minutes more. Then he said evenly, "It's very much my business, Mr. Dugan. Mr. Winslow has hired me to make sure he gets his son back."

"Well, then, I hope you find his son," Cooper told him. "Katie and Andy are my family. I can't see where your guy fits into the picture at all."

Obviously unbothered by Cooper's assurances, Lowell Madison continued casually, "Mr. Winslow and Ms. Brennan were romantically involved some time ago, and the union produced a son who—"

"Oh, I know who you're talking about now," Cooper interrupted, hoping his voice carried just the right amount of oh-yeah-now-I-remember familiarity. "That's the guy Katie met out in Las Vegas not too long after she met me. The rich, married guy, right? The one who kept harping about how his wife didn't understand him, and made all kinds of promises to Katie if she would sleep with him? I remember she used to talk about how much that guy was harassing her all the time."

"Mr. Dugan, I don't think—"

"About how he always came into the diner and bothered her while she was working. Discreetly, of course, so no one else would get suspicious, but he bothered her just the same."

"Mr. Dugan—"

"About how he made sexually explicit remarks and offered her money and material possessions if she would sleep with him."

"Now, Mr. Dugan, you know—"

"About how he actually even offered her money for her baby after she and I conceived Andy."

Whoa, Cooper thought. *Where did* that *come from?* He had no idea what had fired such a colorful idea in his brain, but once germinated, the seed took hold and blossomed beautifully.

"Can you imagine?" he continued quickly. "The guy was nothing more than some immoral scumbag who was actually trying to buy himself a son? That's illegal, right? Big time."

Finally, Lowell Madison seemed interested in what Cooper was saying. His expression changed from one of boredom to one of speculation, and he trained his gaze intently on Cooper's.

"Yeah, Katie and I might have rushed our relationship some," Cooper continued, "and maybe we were irresponsible the night Andy was conceived, but in the heat of the moment, we just didn't think about using any protection. Well, *you* know how it is when two people just get swept away by their passion, right, Lowell?" After a meaningful pause, Cooper added, "Well, maybe not. But we human beings are warm-blooded, as opposed to you reptilian sorts."

Madison eyed Cooper venomously, but said nothing.

"So Andy was a little...oh...unplanned, and Katie kind of panicked once she found out she'd been knocked up. She didn't tell me right away, you know. And I think it just sort of slipped out one day when she was trying to get Winslow off her back. When she told me he'd actually offered her money for her child, because his wife wasn't able to get pregnant ... Well, you could have knocked me over with a feather. Geez, it's amazing the kind of behavior some people are capable of, isn't it? And he seems like such a fine, upstanding pillar of the community, doesn't he?''

Still Madison remained silent and thoughtful-looking. So, feeling as if he were really on a roll, and proud of himself for his very overactive imagination, Cooper continued on blithely.

''Boy, can you imagine what kind of lawsuit something like *that* could have caused? And what the press would have done with it if they got wind of a guy like Winslow first trying to seduce and take advantage of an innocent like Katie, *then,* as if that weren't bad enough, offering to *buy illegally* the child she conceived with the man she really loved? Sheesh.

''Yeah,'' Cooper went on, ''Winslow's one lucky sonofabitch he didn't meet up with me out there. One... lucky...sonofabitch. I woulda beat the hell out of him after the way he went after Katie.''

He met the other man's gaze levelly for a moment, hoping he was getting his point across. Just for good measure, however, he added, ''I'd still beat the hell out of him if I ever met up with him. Know what I mean?''

Lowell Madison eyed Cooper for a moment, clearly not believing a word of what he'd said, nor feeling in any way threatened, but apparently not quite sure how to approach this new development. Finally, he asked, ''Are you saying you're the boy's biological father?''

Cooper nodded. ''Yeah. Says so right on his birth certificate. I'm the only father that kid has ever known.''

''And you're willing to swear to that in a court of law.''

He nodded again. ''That's my story and I'm sticking to it.''

''Let me just see if I understand this correctly, Mr. Dugan.''

''Take all the time you need, Lowell.''

''It is your testimony that you met Ms. Brennan in Las Vegas, and after a brief, whirlwind romance, got her pregnant. Shortly after that time, she met my client, Mr. Winslow, who first approached her with malicious sexual intent, and who, when he discovered her pregnant—and single—status, offered to buy her child illegally, because his wife is infertile.''

Cooper nodded. ''Yeah, that's my testimony. And you can add this to it. Fortunately, Katie has a lot more moral fiber than your boy does. And so do I. When she told me she was pregnant, I told her we should get married. She wasn't sure she wanted to do that, but she agreed to live with me for a year to see how it went. To be honest, Lowell, we've had our ups and downs. But, hey, what couple doesn't, right? Still, I think she's coming around. She wants to do what's best for Andy, just like I do. So I can see the two of us getting married in the not too distant future and having a very happy home life together.''

Madison shook his head almost imperceptibly. ''You're honestly going to stand in front of a judge and tell him that's the truth?''

''Like I said, Lowell, that's my story, and I'm—''

''—sticking to it. Yes, I see.''

''Good.''

''Then I suppose Mr. Winslow and I will see you and Ms. Brennan in court.''

''Sure—just let us know where and when. Oh, if you can find her, that is.''

''Oh, we'll find her.''

Cooper scrubbed a hand over his face and rubbed it negligently across his chest. ''Yeah, well, when you do, could you tell her to bring home some eggs and a gallon of milk and a loaf of bread with her? The cupboard's kinda bare around here.''

Lowell Madison evidently didn't see the humor in the request. So Cooper smiled, hoping that might help the man understand just how seriously he was taking his threat.

"Mr. Dugan, as entertaining as I find it, I know better than to believe your very farfetched story. Mr. Winslow returned to the Chestnut Hill town house he shared with Ms Brennan after a business trip—and after a rather nasty blizzard—to find a man's bloody T-shirt in his kitchen trash can. Because of the small amount of blood, he deduced that it did not belong to a homicidal maniac who had done in Ms. Brennan and the child, but must instead belong to whomever had helped deliver his son during that nasty blizzard."

Cooper's jaw clenched tight, but he said nothing.

"Mr. Winslow also discovered that a bank account he had opened for Ms. Brennan had been, as they say in the vernacular, cleaned out, by none other than Ms. Brennan herself. But that's where the trail went cold. Until we did some digging, and discovered that you are the paramedic who delivered Ms. Brennan's child. We found you by scouring the Philadelphia hospitals until we located the one where Ms. Brennan registered the child's birth. A little more digging led us here to your home."

Cooper narrowed his eyes in annoyance. "Ooo, well, if you're so smart, then you probably also know Ms. Brennan named me as the boy's father."

"Yes, we do know that, as well. But a simple DNA test will prove otherwise."

Cooper nodded. "Yeah, but what judge is going to order one, when I'm perfectly willing to accept paternity? Those things usually only come into play when a guy's trying to *escape* responsibility. I'm not.

"And chew on this, too," he added with a sneer. "Yeah, I'm the one who delivered Katie's baby. But not because I'm a paramedic. Because he's my son."

After a moment's thought, he added, "It happened like this, Lowell. Katie and I had a fight the day before Andy was born, and she ran off to Winslow's Chestnut Hill town house thinking it would make me mad enough to come and get her. Yeah, that's it. And it did make me mad enough to come and get her. Winslow wasn't home, but by that time, the snow was really coming down, so we broke into the place to find shelter from the storm. There was evidence of forced entry at the front door, wasn't there? Like someone had smashed a heavy medical kit down on the door knob?''

Lowell Madison nodded slightly.

Cooper smiled. ''So Katie and I got snowed in, and Andy was born there. I called an ambulance the next morning, and we all arrived at the hospital together. Then Katie filled out every form necessary exactly as she needed to fill it out, including the application for Andy's birth certificate, which, as we both agree, names me as the boy's father.''

Cooper paused for a minute, trying to remember if there was any ground he'd left uncovered that needed covering. Satisfied that he'd done a pretty good job of making sure the gist of the story was there, he looked Madison squarely in the eye again.

''I defy you to prove otherwise,'' he charged the other man. ''Granted, some of the details are still a little fuzzy in my memory, but by the time this thing comes to court, my memory will be flawless. It's mine and Katie's word against Winslow's. Maybe he's high-powered, rich, influential and able to bribe an entire judicial system. But that system better damned well be able to prove that Andy isn't mine and Katie's. You better be able to show beyond a reasonable doubt that that boy doesn't belong with the two of us. The two people who love him more and can care for him better than anyone else in the world.

''Think you can do that, Lowell?'' Cooper needled him further. ''Because Winslow *won't* be able to bribe a jury of mine and Katie's peers, a jury that will more than likely be made up of common folks like ourselves who probably won't much care for rich guys like Winslow.''

Instead of answering the question directly, Madison asked one of his own. "You're willing to raise another man's child as your own son?"

Cooper wanted to say that of course he was willing to raise a child he cared very much about as his own son. Of course he would accept responsibility for Andy. He wanted to ask the man how he could even ask such a stupid question to begin with. Cooper had already told Lowell Madison that Katie and Andy were his family. And although Cooper might be a lot of things, he wasn't a liar. Well, not usually, anyway, he amended when he reconsidered the whopper he'd just told. After all, that had been for a very good cause.

Hell, he was fast growing to love that kid. He'd helped bring Andy into the world, and if he had anything to say about it, he'd be there to see him through each and every one of life's little battles. Screw the biology. Andy would be Cooper's son in every way that was important.

But all he said to the attorney was, "Andy isn't another man's child. He's my son."

Lowell Madison looked thoughtful for a while longer, then tucked his business card back into his jacket pocket. "Well, then, Mr. Dugan, I suppose we both have a vested interest in finding Ms. Brennan and her son."

Cooper nodded slowly. "Yeah, I guess we do."

As he watched the other man turn and make his way down the walk toward a late-model sports car that seemed far too racy for him, Cooper promised himself he would just have to make sure he found Katie and Andy first.

He closed the door and returned to his bedroom to get dressed, and, as always, the thing he noted first was the rocking chair in the corner. Cooper slapped his open palm to his forehead. Of course. How could he have been so stupid? Fortunately for him, he knew exactly where to find Katie and Andy. And fortunately for all of them, he could be there in a heartbeat.

* * *

"Conrad, I know she and Andy are here, so give it up."

"She says she don't wanna see you."

"Well, that's too bad, because I'm not leaving until I get to talk to her."

Cooper and Conrad DiStefano stood eye-to-eye and toe-to-toe at the threshold of the DiStefano home in Haddon Heights, each trying to stare the other down. They both had the safety and welfare of Katie and her son at heart, but neither was willing to concede that the other knew best.

Cooper, however, considered himself to have the upper hand. Because he could and would camp out on the DiStefanos's doorstep until they called the state police to come and get him. And knowing Katie, she had told the older couple at least enough about her situation to keep the law out of it. Hell, she couldn't trust anyone, after all, except—obviously—the DiStefanos, he reminded himself sarcastically. Least of all Cooper Dugan.

"I'm not kidding, Conrad," Cooper assured the other man. "I won't leave until I've seen Katie."

"Like I said, she don't wanna see you."

Cooper expelled an exasperated breath. "You can stay in the room with us, for God's sake. I'm not going to try anything funny. I just want to talk to her."

Conrad eyed him warily, but he relaxed a little, seeming to lose some of his conviction. "You know, I told her she could probably trust you. You don't seem like no creep. But she said she couldn't trust nobody but me and Ginny."

Cooper clenched his jaw tight. There had been a time when Katie had said she couldn't trust anyone but him. What had happened to change that?

Conrad straightened to his full six-foot-plus height. "And I don't betray nobody's trust."

Cooper frowned, straightening to his own six-foot-plus height. "I don't, either."

The two men returned to their silent staring match, until a slight movement behind Conrad caught Cooper's attention. Katie peeked around the older man's shoulder and met Cooper's gaze with an unblinking intensity.

"Hi," she said softly.

"Hi," he replied. "Can we talk?"

She settled a slim hand on Conrad's arm, and he stepped slightly aside. "Um, it's okay, Conrad. I'll talk to him."

Conrad nodded, but didn't move away.

"Can I come in?" Cooper asked.

She shook her head. "No, I—I'll come out there."

"Where's Andy?"

She gazed at him steadily for a moment, clearly still not certain she could trust him. "He's with Ginny," she finally said.

She nodded to Conrad, who moved completely out of her way, then crossed the threshold, stepped past Cooper, and took a seat on the front stoop. Conrad closed the door behind her, but left it a bit ajar.

No doubt so he could hear Katie when she screamed, Cooper thought dismally. He dropped down to sit beside her, as close as he dared, but not close enough to make her feel threatened. In other words, not nearly as close as he would have liked. He inhaled deeply the fresh scent of her, feeling at once reassured and troubled at having her so near again. Only five days had passed since he had last seen her. Five days that felt like a lifetime.

"You look good," he said honestly. "Rested, I mean," he hastened to add. He didn't want to sound as if he were coming on to her, but wondered how he was going to do that when coming on to Katie was a significant part of what was going through his mind. "Relaxed," he added further. "Like you've been eating better and getting more sleep."

She smiled. "Ginny's a great cook. If I stay here much longer, I'm not going to be able to get up from the dining room table. That woman won't let me do anything to help her out around the house. All she'll let me do is sit on the couch with Andy, watching rented videos and doing crosswords." She laughed. "And, of course, she brings me the most mouth-watering canolis just about every hour on the hour."

He nodded, feeling more than a little guilty. He should have been cooking for Katie while she stayed with him, he told himself, not the other way around. And he should have seen to it that she got more rest. Instead, he'd let Katie do everything for herself and her son... and for Cooper, too. Now that he thought about it, he realized he'd failed both mother and child pretty badly while they'd been under his care.

His care? he taunted himself. What care? Here he'd fancied himself responsible for both of them, but what had he done to enforce or illustrate that responsibility? Not much, he conceded. No wonder the two of them had slipped out during the night without a word. They'd probably thought he couldn't care less.

It had only been the day before the two of them had disappeared that Cooper had actually begun to realize just how much care the two of them needed. And it had only been the day before the two of them had disappeared that he'd realized how much he wanted to be the one doing the caring. That he'd realized how much he did care. That he'd realized how empty his life would be without them.

"Katie, I—"

"Cooper, I—"

They started talking as one and stopped as one, then they looked at each other and laughed a little anxiously.

"You first," they chorused, then laughed some more.

"No, you first," Cooper finally got in.

She hesitated a moment, then said softly, "I'm sorry I sneaked out the way I did."

"So am I," he replied as softly. "Why did you?"

Katie hesitated again, still not certain whether or not she could fully trust Cooper. Nevertheless, she didn't see why she shouldn't be honest with him. "Because William came by your apartment that morning."

His expression would have been the same if she had just slapped him with all her might. *"What?"*

She nodded, but dropped her gaze to her hands, which she entwined nervously in her lap. "I got up to feed Andy about five, and I saw William's car pull up outside the apartment."

"How do you know it was his car?"

"It was his car. I know it was."

"Did you see him?"

This time she shook her head. "No. But I know it was him out there." She hugged her arms over herself. "It was creepy. He never got out of the car. Just sat there watching the apartment. Like he knew I was sitting in the living room looking back out at him or something."

"But if he was out there, why didn't he come to the door?"

Katie glanced up. "I don't know. I figured he was just going to wait for me to come out with Andy. Or that maybe he was just going to wait until you left, then come for me and Andy both."

"Or you figured that maybe Winslow and I were working together," he finished for her, looking more forlorn than she had thought a human being could. "And that he was just waiting for me to bring you out to him. That went through your mind, at least, didn't it?"

Instead of answering his question directly, she told him, "I didn't really stop to think, I guess. I just gathered up Andy and left."

"Without telling me," Cooper said quietly.

She nodded silently.

"Because you thought I was the one who told him you were there."

A moment's silence. Then another nod. "Yeah, maybe. I didn't know for sure, but I couldn't take the risk."

"Katie, it wasn't me. I didn't tell Winslow where to find you. How could you think I was capable of something like that?"

She dropped her gaze again, unable to meet the clear green depths of his eyes—eyes that seemed so free of guise or deceit or treachery. "How could I know for sure what you were capable of?" she demanded. "You're the only one who knew where I was. Who else could it have been?"

"Oh, yeah, me and all my neighbors. And anyone else who saw you wander in and out of the apartment the couple of times you left it. How about the lawyer in Mount Laurel? How about the driver of the M bus?" He thrust a thumb over his shoulder. "And the DiStefanos. How the hell do you know it wasn't Conrad who turned you in to your husband?"

"Don't be ridiculous. Conrad couldn't possibly be the one."

"But I could, right?"

She was silent for a moment, then said, "What about the night Andy was born?"

"What about it?"

"You showed up out of nowhere that night, Cooper. Just in time. How can I be sure William didn't hire you to keep an eye on me when he wasn't around, just in case something like Andy's early arrival came about? How do I know you haven't been on his payroll for months? How do I know you're here now for any reason other than to keep tabs on me until William's court case is all sewn up nice and neat?"

Cooper shook his head at her, his expression one of unmistakable disbelief. "I told you. My showing up the night Andy was born was nothing but a coincidence."

"That was some coincidence."

"But still a coincidence."

Katie sighed, no closer to fully understanding the situation now than she had been before. Finally, she told him, "Look, Cooper, for what it's worth, the other night, when William showed up at your place, I really didn't think you were working for him. But I couldn't know for sure. And I couldn't risk Andy's welfare."

"You couldn't trust me."

She shook her head slowly. "No."

"Not even after everything that happened between us."

This time she sighed heavily. "No."

He sighed, too, a disheartening sound. "How about now?"

She looked at him again. "What do you mean?"

"Do you trust me now? Enough to come back to the apartment with me? Enough to know I would never, *ever*, turn you over to Winslow and his lackeys? Enough to know I'll do whatever I have to do to keep you and Andy safe?"

"I—I don't know."

"Will you come home with me, Katie?"

She studied him for a long, long time, taking in the clear eyes, the rigid set of his mouth, the tense, tight muscles of his neck and arms. She told herself there was no way she could believe Cooper capable of doing anything to hurt her or Andy. She told herself he was telling the truth. She told herself she and her son would be perfectly safe as long as she was with Cooper.

Then she told herself that trust was a luxury she just couldn't afford right now. Not as long as Andy's welfare was at stake.

Finally, reluctantly, she shook her head, and saw Cooper deflate like a man left without hope.

"I'm sorry, Cooper," she said quietly. "But I think I'll stay here with Conrad and Ginny."

He nodded, his jaw clenched tight, but he didn't look at her again. "Yeah, well, be careful, because Winslow sent one of his messengers to my apartment today. A guy named Lowell Madison.''

Katie's heart plummeted to her stomach like a cold, hard stone. She knew Lowell Madison. He was one of the few of William's associates that she had met. He wasn't much fun, but he was effective. The fact that Cooper mentioned him verified one of two things. Either he was telling the truth, and William had just sent Madison to Cooper's apartment to find out if she was there. Or else, Cooper already knew Madison from prior dealings with her fake husband, and this just confirmed that he was in fact in William's employ.

''How, um...'' she began cautiously. ''How did Lowell know where to find you?''

Cooper scrubbed a hand over his jaw. ''Winslow found my bloody T-shirt in the garbage at your place in Chestnut Hill and figured out Andy was born at home. He also figured you must have gone to the hospital at some point, and just kept checking until he found the one where Andy's birth was registered. Somebody at St. Teresa's must have told them that I'm the one who arrived in the ambulance with you. Then they went looking for me.''

Katie swallowed hard. She wanted to believe that. She really did. ''What...what did you tell Lowell about me? About Andy? About...about us?''

Cooper chuckled, but there wasn't a humorous note in the sound at all. ''I told him I was Andy's father. I told him you and I had been living together for months. I told him if Winslow even tried to take Andy away from you, he'd have a court battle on his hands like nothing he could ever imagine, and that I'd swear on a stack of whatever literature he wanted to use that you and Andy are my family. Mine.''

Finally, he turned to meet her gaze levelly. ''That's what I told him about us. It's the truth, Katie. Whether you believe it or not is up to you.''

He stood and began to stroll away, but stopped at the edge of the walk and turned around again. ''I would never do anything to hurt you or Andy. I would fight to the death before I would let anyone lay a hand on either one of you. I thought after everything we..." He sighed heavily. "I thought you would have figured that out for yourself by now. But I guess I was wrong."

He turned away again, and Katie watched him make his way down the street, to where he had parked his Jeep. He never turned around to look at her once. He just levered himself up into the vehicle, started the engine with a roar, pulled carefully away from the curb, and sped down the street. The last glimpse she had was of his left turn signal flashing. Then the Jeep—and Cooper—were completely out of sight.

Trust was a precious, precarious thing, she told herself, never to be given lightly. And never to be taken away lightly, either. She had gone to Cooper in the first place because she had been certain he was the only person she could trust. How and why had she forgotten that?

She told herself it was still possible that Cooper could be stopping at a phone booth that very minute to call William and tell him where she and Andy were. Or he could be going back to his apartment, alone. Katie had a decision to make, and any hesitation on her part could cost her dearly.

She could lose her son if she chose unwisely, she reminded herself. Or she could keep her son and lose Cooper. Or, maybe, if she did the right thing, she could have them both forever. But if she did the wrong thing, she reminded herself, she would wind up more alone than she'd ever been in her life. They were high stakes on which to gamble, to be sure. But, oh, what a prize awaited her if she won.

If she won.

Twelve

Katie wasn't surprised to find Cooper at home when she went back to his apartment a little over an hour later. Nor was she surprised that he still appeared to be angry with her. What did surprise her, as she stood at the threshold of his front door with Andy tucked safely in the Snugli against her chest, was that he looked so drained and so tired.

She hadn't noticed it at the DiStefanos's, maybe because she had made every effort during their exchange not to look at Cooper unless she absolutely had to, and then only for a second or two when she did. But now that she gave herself the opportunity to study him more fully, she realized he looked like a man who had gone days without any kind of human interaction and nights without any kind of sleep.

"Are you still speaking to me?" she asked without preamble.

His eyes cleared some of their troubling intensity, but he continued to look anxious about something. "Of course I'm still speaking to you."

She hesitated a moment, then asked, "Can I come in?"

Immediately, he stepped aside, sweeping his hand toward the interior of the apartment with all the grace of an overpaid butler. "Yeah, sure. I just wasn't sure you'd want to. I figured you might be worried you'd find William Winslow and his all-suit orchestra in there waiting to pounce on you and your son."

She nibbled her lip nervously for a moment, then took a step toward him. "No, I'm not worried about that."

"You're worried about something," he said as she made her way past him.

Silently, he pushed the front door closed after her, then leaned back against it, as if fearful she would change her mind and bolt from his life once again.

She said nothing in response to his statement, just reached to her sides to unfasten the Snugli. "Would you mind holding Andy for a few minutes? My back is beginning to hurt."

His expression changed significantly then, from one of hot resentment to one of warm affection. "Yeah, sure, I'll hold the little guy."

Katie relinquished her son to Cooper's care, and smiled when she saw the absolute joy that overcame both of them once the exchange was complete. Cooper hefted Andy to hold him close to his shoulder, and Andy reached out a tiny hand to tweak Cooper's nose. Both of them smiled at the gesture, Cooper punctuating his delight further with a quick chuckle.

"Good to see you again, kid," he said quietly. "The old place hasn't been the same without you." His gaze trained quickly from the baby to Katie. "Or your mom."

Before Katie could respond, Andy blew a wet raspberry and cooed his own pleasure at seeing Cooper again. Then the nand that gripped his nose splayed open over Cooper's cheek. Cooper lifted his own hand to gently cover the tiny one, and he tilted his head to place a soft kiss on the baby's cheek. Andy's smile broadened, and he made a soft, satisfied sound.

"Yeah, this place has been way too quiet without you and your mom," Cooper told the baby. "No jazzy dance tunes in the afternoon, no hungry howling at all hours, no splashing in the dishpan during bath time, no ridiculous baby talk, no Gershwin in the night. No fun at all." He turned to gaze at Katie, but still looked a little sad, a little uncertain. "It's good to have you both back. I do have you both back, don't I? That's what this is all about, I hope."

As Katie considered the two of them, her heart turned over. How could she possibly have ever suspected that Cooper would do anything to harm her or Andy? He had nothing at all in common with William. The two were beyond comparison.

From the moment she had met her phony husband, Katie had harbored some misgivings about him. Some strange, indistinct something that had continuously nudged at the back of her brain and completely defied definition. But she'd been so flattered by his attentions, so dazzled by his wealth, so charmed by his kindness, that she had forced herself to ignore the doubts that provoked her whenever William was around. She was so happy to have found something she thought was stable and permanent, so delighted to think that her life was finally going to be complete, that she had told herself she was being silly to be suspicious.

But for some reason, she had never stopped being suspicious. Her doubts about her husband had never gone away. In spite of everything, she had never been entirely comfortable about her marriage.

But Cooper had felt comfortable since the moment she had met him. Even without knowing a thing about him, Katie had somehow sensed he was a good guy. A decent human being. The kind of man a woman could trust implicitly. She'd never had doubts about Cooper until the morning William had shown up outside the apartment. And those had been brought about by panic, not by any real evidence that contradicted what she knew to be true about Cooper.

And what she knew to be true about Cooper was that she could trust him. No matter what. She didn't know why or how she had forgotten that. But it would never happen again.

She watched with a warm feeling that spread from her heart to her toes as he moved to the sofa and sat down, cupping his hands under Andy's armpits and settling the baby's feet on his own thighs, so that the baby stood face-to-face with him.

"You look good, kid," he told the infant. "I think you've grown an inch and gained a pound since you and your mom skipped out on me."

"Cooper, I'm sorry about that. I—"

"Don't apologize," he said without looking away from the baby. "You were thinking about Andy. Hell, I probably would have done the same thing in your shoes."

"No, you wouldn't."

He looked up at her then, his eyes never leaving hers, but he said nothing.

"You would have trusted me," Katie told him. "In spite of growing up in a situation where you have every reason to distrust people and push them away, you would have trusted me. You would have kept me and Andy close."

He continued to study her, but still remained silent.

"It's what makes you so..." She shrugged a little self-consciously. "So...trustworthy, Cooper. There's just some kind of inbred decency in you that no amount of bad life experience could whip out of you. William came from a privileged background and presents a perfectly respectable front, yet he's done some things that go beyond mean and vicious. But you..."

She inhaled deeply and moved to sit beside Cooper on the couch. She cupped Andy's cheek with one hand and Cooper's with the other. Then she smiled.

"You," she went on, "someone who has every reason to be mean and vicious, you've got a tender, caring streak in you a mile wide. I was just too foolish and frightened to see it."

She dropped her hand from his face, then leaned forward and kissed the cheek she had held, lightly, quickly, almost fearful that he would push her away when she did.

But Cooper didn't push her away. Instead, when she drew back from him, he turned his head and leaned forward again to claim her mouth with his own, hard and fast. Then he pulled away, tucked Andy into his lap and supported him with one arm, then looped his other arm around Katie's neck and urged her forward once more.

This time when he kissed her, he took his time. He traced the outline of her mouth with the tip of his tongue, then tugged her bottom lip into his mouth with a gentle suction. When Katie parted her lips to moan out loud, he gently guided his tongue past them, tasting her fully, exploring her completely. She lifted her hands to frame his face, pulling him closer before driving her fingers into the soft silk of his hair.

Only a soft protest from Andy halted what might have become a truly earth-shattering experience. Katie and Cooper eased away from each other at the same time, both of them smiling, both of them trying with some difficulty to steady their ragged breathing. But Cooper still clenched a fistful of her hair in one hand, and Katie continued to cup his cheek in her palm.

"I don't know how I could have doubted you," she said softly. "I guess I just went a little crazy for a while."

He grinned at her. "I've felt a little crazy since the day I met you," he said with a small laugh.

She laughed, too. "Yeah, well, under the circumstances..."

"I guess most people do follow a more traditional route to get to know each other. Like maybe having dinner or seeing a movie, or at least learning a little bit about each other, before they bring a baby into the world together."

"Well, who are we to follow tradition?"

Cooper's smile broadened. "It's never been one of my strong suits, anyway."

"Then I guess we'll just have to start a few of our own traditions."

The minute Katie made the statement, she regretted it. In spite of everything, she supposed she was making presumptions she had no business making. Yes, she and Cooper were certainly on the road to something special. But there still hadn't been any mention made of love or forever after. And there was still the small business of William Winslow to get settled.

"I'm sorry," she said quickly, "I didn't mean—"

"Katie," Cooper interrupted her. "Don't apologize."

"But I didn't mean for that to sound the way it did."

"And how did it sound to you?"

"Like I had already measured and fitted you up to be perfect husband and father material."

"That's what it sounded like to me, too."

"I'm sorry. I—"

"And just what's so awful about that?"

"Just that..." She halted quickly when she realized he didn't seem to be offended by her proprietary stand on him. "What do you mean, 'What's so awful about that?'"

"Just what I said. What's so awful about you sizing me up for the roles of husband and father?"

"Well, just...I didn't think you wanted to be anyone's husband or father."

He shook his head and laughed some more. "I've said it before, Katie, and I'll say it again. I'm Andrew's rightful father. It says so on his birth certificate."

"But—"

"Hey, I even remember the night Andy was conceived, and I'll be more than happy to describe it in detail to every court in the country."

"But, Cooper—"

"It was summer in Nevada," he went on before she could stop him, "and I was out there, just passing through, because it was the kind of place I'd always wanted to visit."

"Cooper, you don't have to do—"

"I met a wonderful woman out there in Nevada, too," he continued, obviously warming to his story.

Katie relented and kept silent as he stared out at the room, convinced he was seeing something else entirely, and not altogether certain she wanted to obstruct his view.

As if he'd forgotten she was there, he continued in a dreamy, faraway voice, "Yeah, I met a wonderful woman out there in Nevada. This great-looking, fun-loving waitress, and it was love at first sight. For both of us. One night, we went for a drive. The desert is a beautiful place that time of year, Your Honor, and we found this nice, quiet, little romantic spot, then parked to enjoy the scenery. I kissed Katie for the first time under a blanket of stars. One thing led to another, and, well . . . You know how it goes, Judge. Nine months later, my little namesake was born."

"Oh, Cooper . . ."

"So you can imagine our shock and horror, Your Honor, when Mr. Winslow offered to buy the baby from Katie once he found out she was pregnant and single."

Katie opened her mouth to say something, then, when Cooper's statement fully registered in her brain, forgot immediately what she had planned to say. "When he *what?*"

Cooper nodded and smiled. "Yeah, it's just a little something I whipped up on the spur of the moment when Lowell Madison was here."

She tapped an index finger against her lip and studied him for a long moment. Finally, she said, "Um, I think you'd better be a little more specific."

As quickly as he could, Cooper reiterated what he had told Lowell Madison about his and Katie's fictitious situation—man, woman and child. He stressed the part about it being their word against Winslow's and the part about the two of them and their son being one big happy family. And, feeling suddenly more gregarious than he ever had in his life, he even added a charitable comment about William Winslow.

"Still, Your Honor," he continued his make-believe plea to the justice system, "maybe in that weird, psychotic brain of Winslow's—and he is clearly psychotic, Judge, if he's running around offering to buy unborn babies, so you might want to rule for one of those psychological evaluations— maybe he thinks he's helping Katie out by making up this cockamamy story about the two of them being romantically involved and saying that Andy is his. Maybe he thinks taking the baby off her hands for him and his wife to raise will help her get a new lease on life.

"But that would be a terrible thing, wouldn't it, Your Honor, letting someone be responsible for a baby who didn't really love that child? A baby should be with the people who care about him, shouldn't he? A baby should be with the people who love him. Because love, that's what makes a parent, you know? Not chromosomes, not who was there when the child was conceived. It's the love that a parent gives that's important. Don't you think so?"

Cooper paused for only a moment, only long enough to meet Katie's gaze again. "That's why, Your Honor, I'm ready to act like a man and do the right thing. The time has come for me to face up to my responsibilities and marry the mother of my child. Hey, I love them, after all, and couldn't live without Katie or my son.''

For a long time, Katie could say nothing. Because she realized to her amazement that Cooper was dead serious. When he'd offered to marry her before, she'd known the suggestion was off-the-cuff, that no thought on his part had gone into it at all. But this time...this time he had obviously done some serious planning. This time, he had every intention of carrying through with it.

Her mind reeled at the proposition. A mixture of relief and terror welled up inside her, warring with the already confounded feelings she had for Cooper. What he was suggesting would be impossible. Of that she was certain. It was all founded on dishonesty and deceit, and no good could come of it in the end. The enormity of the lie overwhelmed her. As if it weren't enough that he was offering to marry her and legitimize Andy as his own son. He certainly didn't have to say that he loved her.

Unless, maybe, he did.

''You've, um...you've given this a lot of thought, haven't you?'' she asked.

''Some,'' he conceded.

''Just when did you formulate such an elaborate plan?''

''The elaborate plan part came up while I was talking to Lowell Madison. I don't know exactly *where* it came from....'' he added with a chuckle. ''Maybe it was destiny filling my head with wild ideas, but it might just work.''

''And the marriage part?'' she asked. ''Just how long have you been entertaining *that* wild idea?''

''The marriage part sort of took root the day you got back from seeing that lawyer in Mount Laurel. When I saw the way your face changed at the thought of losing Andy.''

She smiled sadly. ''You're sweet, Cooper. And I'm touched by your gesture. But I can't let you do this. I can't let you ruin your life by going along with a bogus marriage.

You're not responsible for Andy or me. There's no way I'm going to—"

"That's where you're wrong, Katie," he interrupted her. "I *am* responsible. For Andy *and* you. I have been since the day he was born. Maybe I haven't been showing it very well but that's about to change. Call it karma, call it kismet, call it crazy, but..." He laughed a little anxiously. "As much as it embarrasses me to admit I believe in such a thing...it's destiny, that's what it is. I *am* responsible for the two of you. More than that, I *love* the two of you."

"Cooper, please. You don't have to lie to me. I'm a big girl. I can take—"

"I'm not lying, Katie. I've never been more honest about anything in my life. Hell, maybe I've never been honest about anything in my life. Until now. Until this."

He draped the arm that wasn't holding Andy over her shoulder and stroked his open palm up and down her bare arm, as if doing so might help to emphasize what he had to say. "Having you and Andy around—even for such a short time—made me realize how much I've been missing. I never really stopped to consider how hollow my life is. But when you get right down to it, there's nothing to it. I get up in the morning, I go to work, I come home and I sleep.

"Okay, I save a few lives here and there," he conceded with a grin. "But what have I done lately to save my own life? Nothing. Not until I took you and Andy in."

"You were saving *our* lives, Cooper. We weren't saving yours," Katie corrected him.

"Oh, no. Opening my door to you was a purely selfish gesture. Trust me. When I saw you standing there, I realized how much I had missed you since that night, and how badly I wanted you in my life, whether you were married to someone else or not. And since then, you and Andy have shown me what's really important. What makes the difference between existing on a planet and living on it. And..."

He sighed fitfully, but his smile grew broader. "I guess you could say I love you for it."

"I love you, too." The words were out before she consciously chose to say them. And without even thinking about what else she was feeling, she continued, "I didn't think I'd ever be able to trust anyone again after what William did to me. But something about you, Cooper, just feels so...I don't know. So right. I felt it the minute you showed up that night in Chestnut Hill. It was weird. But nice. You know?"

He nodded silently and smiled down at her, then drew her close, tucking her head beneath his chin, holding her body close to his to illustrate just what a perfect fit the two of them were.

"Maybe it is karma or kismet," she went on with a small chuckle. "And maybe it is crazy. But you're right. My destiny does lie with you. Mine and Andy's both."

"So what are we going to do about it?" she heard him ask, his voice low and full of affection.

Katie sighed heavily. "I don't know. No matter what happens between the two of us, we still have William to deal with. William and his twisted sense of ownership. William and his pin-striped army of suits. William and his best-buddy judges who will do exactly what he tells them to do, as long as the price is right. Even if we do stick to that story of yours, even if it means committing perjury..."

She couldn't quite quell the shudder that wound through her at the thought of engaging in such a serious crime, even if it was for the sake of her child. She lifted her head from Cooper's chest and tilted it back to meet his gaze. "You tell me. So what are we going to do about it?"

Without hesitation, he smiled and told her, "We'll see him in court."

"What do you mean?"

"I mean William doesn't have a legal leg to stand on, what with me named as Andy's father on the birth certificate and more than willing to concede the fact of my paternity under oath.''

Katie's stomach knotted in worry at the thought of Cooper doing such a thing, at the thought of the two of them guilty of a felony, regardless of how noble the intentions. ''But I can't let you do that. I can't let you lie in a court of law. It's illegal.''

''Katie, it will never get that far. Unless Winslow wants to create a situation that would instigate a number of long drawn-out lawsuits that would probably get him nowhere it will be pointless for him to take us to court. There's nothing he can do unless he wants to try his hand at kidnapping.''

Katie felt herself go pale. Of everything she'd considered about William and his appallingly amoral character, the idea that he might actually kidnap Andy had never entered her mind. Until now.

She clutched Cooper's shirtfront frantically. ''Oh, God Cooper, I hadn't even thought of that. What if he does try something like that?''

Cooper smiled again, a decidedly evil smile, full of mischief and mayhem.

''Cooper?'' Katie asked. ''Why are you looking at me like that?''

He wiggled his eyebrows expressively. ''Like I said, we'll see him in court. But not for long. Because it won't take any time at all to convict him. Then we can watch him through the bars of a paddy wagon as they cart him off to jail. Granted, it will probably only be a minimum security facility where he can learn to grow marigolds for the next twenty or thirty years, but he'll still be locked up good and tight.''

She narrowed her eyes at him suspiciously. ''What are you talking about? How can you be so sure he'd even be caught let alone convicted? I thought it was my word against his. And, even if he was convicted, why would he go to a minimum security prison for kidnapping?''

Cooper hugged her close again, giving her a quick squeeze before releasing her. "Oh, it won't be kidnapping he'll be convicted of. He won't have the opportunity for that. Didn't I tell you? He's been siphoning money from his employer for about eight years now. More than three million bucks."

"He's done *what?*"

Cooper nodded vigorously. "You remember that night I told you I had to go out and not to wait up for me? That there was somebody I needed to see?"

Katie nodded. How could she forget that? It had been part of what spurred her unfounded suspicions.

"Well, I saw a couple of acquaintances I have in the...uh...the law enforcement field. They got back to me yesterday and told me some pretty interesting things about Winslow."

"Like what?"

Cooper's expression was smug and satisfied as he told her, "Seems he and his company have had some dealings with certain heads of governments that are big no-nos where the great United States of America is concerned. Selling them all kinds of things to make weapons that would be used against U.S. soldiers. Uncle Sam really does tend to frown on that kind of thing. Winslow is just one of a number of executives who are going to be arrested. I guess that old saying about no honor among thieves is right. Not only has the guy been a traitor to his country, he's been stealing money from his partners in crime."

Katie could only stare for a moment. Then she said, "I reiterate. He's done *what?*"

Cooper's smile broadened. "Yeah, William Winslow's not the only one who has friends in high places," he said. "My acquaintances looked into Mr. Winslow's past and discovered more than a few unseemly things about the guy's character. Or lack thereof. Turns out your fake husband has been under investigation for some time now, and the feds are *this* close to putting him away for a good, long time. Pretty neat, huh?''

Katie could say nothing. She felt weak and wary and wonderful. It seemed too simple. Too easy. Too tidy. She didn't doubt for a moment that William was guilty of everything Cooper had described. She just couldn't quite believe her good fortune.

"Like I said," he told her, "he'll be in jail for a long, long time. Certainly long enough for Andy to grow to adulthood and decide for himself what makes a good father.''

Cooper pulled Katie close again and kissed her soundly, softly, then looked down at the baby in his arms. "And I intend to be a very good father to our son. And to any other kids we might have along the way. It may have taken me a while to realize it, but it's not the genetic material inside a man that makes him a father, is it?''

Katie smiled and shook her head. "No. It's that intangible bit of daddiness that some guys have and some guys don't. You, Cooper, just happen to have it by the truckloads.''

"Lucky for me you chose the right guy to be Andy's father.''

"Or maybe it *was* destiny that stepped in that snowy night.''

"And, hey, who can argue with destiny?''

"Not me.''

"Me, neither.''

The sound of a very loud raspberry piped up from somewhere below, and Katie and Cooper turned to find Andy staring and smiling at them in utter approval.

Katie laughed. "I guess Andy doesn't want to argue with destiny, either.''

"Hmm," Cooper murmured. "I was sort of under the impression the little guy *was* destiny.''

"Yeah, I guess in a lot of ways he is." She smiled at her son. At their son. "Thanks, Andy," she said softly.

''Sthuputhubb,'' he replied eloquently with a generous smile in return.

Katie and Cooper laughed in unison and held each other tighter, she feeling good to be part of a family again, he feeling grateful to have found one at last. And both quite certain that the future held nothing but the promise of a happy life together. Forever.

It was, after all, their destiny.

Epilogue

―――――

"Okay, Andy, we're ready."

"No, we're not. I'm out of tape."

"Okay, Andy, wait a minute. Wait 'til your father gets the video camera loaded again. Okay, now. No, wait! Not yet. Okay... now! Blow out the candles, sweetie!"

"Mo-om, will you puh-leeze quit talking to me like I'm a kid?"

"I'm sorry, honey, I didn't mean to. But you know how your father and I like to get these things on record for the Dugan Family Video Vault. You only turn thirteen once, you know."

"Thank God for that."

"Don't you use that tone of voice with me, young man."

"Yeah, leave Mommy alone, Andy!"

"Yeah, Andy! Leave Mommy alone!"

"Yeah, don't you talk to Mommy that way, Andy!"

"Don't start with me, pip-squeaks. I can take all three of you on at once and still walk away clean."

"Andy, please. Just blow out the candles like your mother asked, okay? I think I've got it now."

"Yeah, yeah, yeah. Dad?"

"What?"

"The lens cap is still on."

"Oh. Sorry. Got it. Ready now. Go ahead."

"Okay, everybody, stand clear. Andy's going to blow out his birthday candles."

"I'll help, Andy!"

"Me, too!"

"Me, too, Andy! I wanna help!"

"You had to have three more, didn't you, Mom? Why couldn't you just let me be an only child?"

"Ahem. Well, actually Andy, there is something your father and I need to tell you all."

"Oh, no. The last time you said that, six months later, Megan showed up."

"Yes, we know, but . . . um . . ."

"Oh, Mom . . . Not another one."

"Andy, your mother and I thought you'd be pleased. What with three sisters, we thought you might want a shot at a little brother."

"Dad, you've got to be kidding."

"Hey, we're outnumbered two to one here, kid. This would even the odds."

"It, um . . . it would appear that I'm carrying twins, Andy."

"Yay! Mommy's going to have more babies!"

"Yay! We get to live in a bigger house!"

"Yay! I don't have to be the baby anymore!"

"Twins! Mo-om! You can't be serious! Cripes, what are you guys trying to do? Beat Conrad and Ginny's record?"

"Hey, kiddo, you leave me and Ginny outta this."

"Sorry, Conrad."

"No problem, kiddo."

"It's just . . . you know . . . six kids?"

"Hey, at least you've got your own room, Andy. That's more than Steffie and I have."

"Button it, Nikki. If Mom and Dad keep this up, none of us are going to have any room. Mom, how could you?"

"Oh, stop it, Andy. We need a bigger house anyway. I've got so many voice students now, I need to expand the studio. We'll stay in Pennsauken—you won't even have to change schools. I'm sure Melody Applebaum will be happy to hear that."

"Mo-om, Melody Applebaum is gross."

"Uh-huh. That's why you spend an hour talking to her on the phone every night."

"Mo-om..."

"And this way, you can all have your own rooms. Just think how close we'll all be, sweetie. I think it's wonderful having such a big family. Now, be honest. Don't you agree? Don't you like having siblings?"

"Hmpf. Well...I guess it won't be so bad having another couple more around. As long as you promise you've got at least one boy in there."

"I'm afraid that's up to your father, sweetie."

"Dad?"

"I did my best, kid. I guess we'll just have to wait and see what happens."

"Yeah, yeah, yeah. Oh, gross, not again. Will you quit the kissing already? Take it outside, for crying out loud. On second thought, don't. No telling what the neighbors would say. Sheesh."

"Oh, Andy. Happy birthday, sweetie."

"Thanks, Mom."

"Thirteen years old. It doesn't seem like any time at all has passed since you were born. Now that was a night to remember, wasn't it, Cooper?"

"You got that right, Katie. You got that right."

"Not again, Mom, please. We've all heard this story before a million times. A miracle in a snowstorm, right?"

"Right."

"The night Dad came to save us both from oblivion, right?"

"Right."

"The knight in shining armor saves the damsel in distress and her kid from the fire-breathing dragon that might have wound up being his father, right?"

"Right."

"And Lewis Prentiss, attorney extraordinaire, friend of the Dugan family and all-around nice guy—"

"Uh, yeah, that would be me."

"Right. Lewis steps in to drive the final nails in the dragon's coffin, right?"

"Right."

"In other words, Mom, it was destiny, right?"

"Right."

"And true love won out, right?"

"Right."

"Oh, for... will you stop it with the kissing again?"

"Andy?"

"What?"

"Blow out your candles already."

"Yeah, yeah, yeah..."

*   *   *   *   *

The exciting new cross-line continuity series about love,
marriage—and Daddy's unexpected need for a baby
carriage!

It all began with *THE BABY NOTION*
by Dixie Browning (Desire #1011 7/96)

And the romance in New Hope, Texas, continues with:

BABY IN A BASKET
by Helen R. Myers (Romance #1169 8/96)

Confirmed bachelor Mitch McCord finds a baby on
his doorstep and turns to lovely gal-next-door
Jenny Stevens for some lessons in fatherhood—and love!

Don't miss the upcoming books in this wonderful series:

MARRIED...WITH TWINS!
by Jennifer Mikels (Special Edition#1054, 9/96)

HOW TO HOOK A HUSBAND (AND A BABY)
by Carolyn Zane (Yours Truly #29, 10/96)

DISCOVERED: DADDY
by Marilyn Pappano (Intimate Moments #746, 11/96)

DADDY KNOWS LAST continues
each month...only from

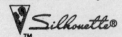

DKL-R

As seen on TV!
Free Gift Offer

With a Free Gift proof-of-purchase from any Silhouette® book,
you can receive a beautiful cubic zirconia pendant.

This gorgeous marquise-shaped stone is a genuine cubic
zirconia—accented by an 18" gold tone necklace.

(Approximate retail value $19.95)

Send for yours today...
compliments of ▼ *Silhouette®*
TM

To receive your free gift, a cubic zirconia pendant, send us one original proof-of-
purchase, photocopies not accepted, from the back of any Silhouette Romance™
Silhouette Desire®, Silhouette Special Edition®, Silhouette Intimate Moments®
or Silhouette Yours Truly™ title available in August, September or October at your favorite
retail outlet, together with the Free Gift Certificate, plus a check or money order for
$1.65 u.s./$2.15 can. (do not send cash) to cover postage and handling, payable
to Silhouette Free Gift Offer. We will send you the specified gift. Allow 6 to 8 weeks for
delivery. Offer good until October 31, 1996 or while quantities last. Offer valid in the
U.S. and Canada only.

Free Gift Certificate

Name: _____

Address: _____

City: _____ State/Province: _____ Zip/Postal Code: _____

Mail this certificate, one proof-of-purchase and a check or money order for postage
and handling to: SILHOUETTE FREE GIFT OFFER 1996. In the U.S.: 3010 Walden
Avenue, P.O. Box 9077, Buffalo NY 14269-9077. In Canada: P.O. Box 613, Fort Erie
Ontario L2Z 5X3.

FREE GIFT OFFER   084-KMD
ONE PROOF-OF-PURCHASE
To collect your fabulous FREE GIFT, a cubic zirconia pendant, you must include this
original proof-of-purchase for each gift with the properly completed Free Gift Certificate.

084-KMD

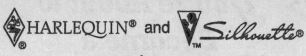

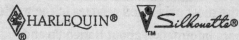

You're About to Become a *Privileged Woman*

Reap the rewards of fabulous free gifts and benefits with proofs-of-purchase from Silhouette and Harlequin books

Pages & Privileges™

It's our way of thanking you for buying our books at your favorite retail stores.

PROOF OF PURCHASE
SD-PP164
Offer expires October 31, 1996

**Harlequin and Silhouette—
the most privileged readers in the world!**

For more information about Harlequin and Silhouette's PAGES & PRIVILEGES program call the Pages & Privileges Benefits Desk: 1-503-794-2499

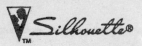

Silhouette®

SD-PP164